A Sweet Love

A Christmas Story

Caroline McIntosh

To all those who love Christmas

Contents

Chapter One

♥

Thirteen days until Christmas

D orothy pulled the café door closed. She had twenty seconds to lock it before the alarm went wild. Despite having done it for years, she hated locking up her café. But she had to keep her sweet treats safe.

It was six o'clock in the evening. Darkness had descended, and only one other person was out: Oliver Livingstone, the elderly owner of the local bookshop. Dorothy heard the jangle of his keys as he unlocked the door to his flat above the bookshop.

Fifteen seconds.

Dorothy cursed. It wasn't just the jangle of keys that distracted her. Another noise spoiled the quiet air. The loud roar of a car's engine.

Ten seconds.

Dorothy concentrated on the lock. Quickly, she turned the key and it fit into place. She pulled it from the lock and waited for confirmation that the alarm was on.

'System set,' she heard the mechanical voice say through the glass door.

Satisfied, Dorothy tucked her keys into her pocket.

The roar of the car's engine had morphed into a purr now. Then, an unfamiliar voice spoke. Rough, with a lilt. There was something intriguing about the sound.

Dorothy's eyebrows knitted together as she heard Oliver respond. What was going on?

A duty of protection visited Dorothy. She wanted to be sure that Oliver got inside safely. She walked down the pavement and her face scrunched in concern as she asked, 'Oliver, are you alright?'

The voice from the car stopped and the window rolled up. Dorothy looked but couldn't see anyone inside due to the blacked-out window.

'What was that about?' Dorothy asked just as the car squealed into a U-turn.

'Oh, someone was lost,' Oliver replied. 'He was heading for the Baileys'.'

The engine noise puffed into the distance as the car took a right turn.

'Goodness!' Dorothy said. 'It didn't need to be that loud, did it?'

Oliver chuckled. 'If you don't mind, Dorothy, I need to rest for the evening.'

'Of course,' Dorothy said, a sense of protectiveness still with her. 'Will you be alone?'

Oliver stilled as he opened the door to his home. 'Dorothy, I might be eighty but I'm perfectly capable of looking after myself. Thank you very much.' He tapped his cane on the ground to enforce his point.

He sounded tired and Dorothy wondered if his son and daughter-in-law had already had this conversation with him.

'I'm sorry, Oliver. The car surprised me, that's all.' She stepped away from him. 'Good night. I'll see you tomorrow.'

With that, she crossed the road and began down Butterfly Lane. She considered stopping to search through her handbag as an excuse to look back and be sure that Oliver had got into his house safely, but there was no need; she heard the gentle click of a door closing.

Chapter Two

♥

Countdown Day 1

Twelve days until Christmas

Dorothy had signed her café up to participate in the Christmas Countdown marketing campaign: a set of activities designed by the Lavender Village Committee to promote local businesses in the days leading up to Christmas. People who took part would be rewarded with a stamp for each activity they participated in, with the winners receiving various prizes.

Lavender Village Café was hosting two or three events, including offering a Festive Special: whenever a customer bought a hot drink, they had the option to also purchase a mug, which came stuffed with three biscuits – two gingerbread men and one orange biscuit. She'd chosen the orange biscuit because it was their most popular item.

After counting thirty such packages and making sure the biscuits were perfectly set in the mugs, an idea sprung into her head. Perhaps she'd take one to Oliver at the bookshop to see how he was doing.

'May!' she called from the back of the shop. 'I'm just popping out.'

She didn't have to announce it, since she was the boss, but she liked her employees to know when she wasn't on the premises.

Dorothy hurried to the bookshop, opening the large wooden door to be greeted by several familiar faces: Oliver, who was wearing one of his friendly smiles, and his son Stephen and daughter-in-law Abigail.

'Oh, hello,' Dorothy said with a smile. 'I haven't interrupted anything, have I?'

'No,' Abigail replied kindly. She was one of Dorothy's good friends.

'Dorothy!' Oliver greeted. 'It's lovely to see you this morning. We're just preparing to open our doors for today.'

Dorothy felt his kindness. It was as if Oliver had forgotten their strange interaction yesterday evening. But then Oliver usually held everyone in high regard, and he was quick to forget past concerns.

'I remember the chair...' a disembodied voice spoke at the back of the shop.

A northerner? Welsh? Dorothy tried to figure out where the accent was from.

'Oliver, do you...' A tall, solid man appeared at the end of the aisle, speech trailing off as he noticed Dorothy standing there. 'Hello,' he said, looking directly at her.

She shivered. Was the door open? She was sure the temperature had dropped.

'Philip,' Stephen said as he walked towards the man, 'this is Dorothy. One of Abigail's friends.'

As Dorothy watched the tall man approach her, a strange feeling visited her. One she hadn't felt for a very long time.

'Hello,' she managed. She wasn't sure how. She swallowed, her gaze travelling up and down his person. She noted his sturdy body hidden by his jeans, cotton top and open green coat. He had short dark hair and a slight beard which, for some inexplicable reason, she wanted to touch.

Then her gaze reached his eyes – burning dark navy with twinges of green in them. Dorothy wasn't sure she'd ever seen eyes so intriguing.

'Dorothy,' the man came closer, repeating her name as if trying to memorise it. His large hand clasped hers and the shivery feeling wrapped around her as they touched. She blinked to understand it, to no avail.

'Philip's visiting Lavender Village for Christmas,' Abigail explained, a curious look on her face. 'He's taking a break from the big city, Manchester.'

'Oh, right.' Dorothy's mind couldn't keep up with her tongue. 'When did you arrive?'

'Last night,' he responded with a smile, then turned to Oliver. 'That chair is pristine. The oak is in very good condition. How old is it?'

'For all the things that were going on at that time, it's actually hard to say,' Abigail answered. 'Steam trains, rocking chairs…'

The lights in the shop flashed, as if sending them a message. Dorothy looked up in confusion, but they settled back on seconds later.

Oliver kept the flow of the conversation going as if nothing had happened. 'We keep the oak pristine. It's very important to care for the wood.'

'I can see that.' The force of Philip's voice made everyone turn to him. 'I remember it from when I visited once. I believe it was your aunt's birthday. We did a day trip.' Philip looked at Stephen as if to jog his memory.

Abigail stared, wide-eyed. Stephen's eyebrows knitted and Oliver looked as if he was cataloguing something or trying to hear a whispered message.

'Philip's staying in the village for a bit, until after Christmas,' Abigail explained. 'He went to university with Stephen.'

'He's seen the chair over the years,' Oliver said.

'Oh, right,' Dorothy replied, confused by the focus on the chair.

Suddenly a flash of her own childhood popped into her head, and she blinked it away, wondering where that had come from. Then she remembered she had something in her hand.

'Oh, Oliver, I came bearing gifts.' She felt her face redden as she smiled awkwardly. 'Well, for you. I wasn't expecting a crowd.'

Oliver took the gift: one of the mugs filled with biscuits. 'I'll enjoy these,' he said. 'Thank you.'

'We're coming to your café for lunch,' Abigail said.

'Oh, lovely,' Dorothy acknowledged. Then she realised something: Philip had been the one in the car last night. She turned to him. 'You arrived last night?'

'Yeah.' He nodded. 'Got a bit lost, even with Google directions. Long journey, too. You don't do suppers?'

'Sorry?'

'At the café,' Abigail supplied. 'You don't offer supper or evening food.'

'No.' Dorothy said. 'Haven't done for years. There wasn't enough demand.'

'I didn't know where to eat. Google showed the café, but it was closed,' Philip commented.

'What did you do?' Dorothy felt keen to know the answer, though she wasn't sure why.

'Fish and chips. The Baileys ordered some.' Bailey's B&B was a touch further up the road. They were the most welcoming couple who loved to help their guests in any way they could.

'Ah,' Dorothy said, feeling strangely awkward that her café hadn't been open for supper. 'Well, I better head back.'

The last word slowed as yet another feeling visited her. She wasn't sure she wanted to leave just yet, so it was a relief when Abigail stalled her.

'Hang on,' Abigail said, 'how did you know Philip arrived last night?'

'I heard his car when I was locking up,' Dorothy said. She wanted to explain how scared she had felt, but that didn't feel like the right way to describe it. Besides, that feeling had gone away. Now she kept finding herself transfixed by the man's eyes.

'We were just talking about the Christmas Countdown,' Stephen said. 'And how we'll all be taking part in the activities.'

'Oh.' Dorothy looked at Stephen, noticing how much he looked like his father with those twinkly eyes. What was going on with her today? 'You can't, can you? I thought shop owners weren't allowed. You know, most contests don't allow the hosts to take part...?'

She thought of the pile of papers on her desk, the ones about the Christmas Countdown she should have read properly. Instead, she'd skimmed a few paragraphs, signed them and returned them to the committee, along with the payment.

'Twelve days, twelve activities and prompts,' Abigail said. 'Each time you do one, you get a stamp.' She pointed to the large ink pad on the counter. 'For those who are more tech savvy, there's a QR code to use.' She pointed to the paper with the QR code stuck on the end of the bookshelves closest to them.

'Are all twelve things in Lavender Village?' Philip asked.

Dorothy figured this conversation might be helpful to her, since the Countdown started today.

'No, there is one in Sprawling Green, the closest town. It's a few miles from here,' Oliver said. 'It was meant to be just our village, but when Sprawling Green got wind of the plan they got upset and wanted in on the fun, too.' Oliver knew this as he'd been on the planning committee. 'We told them only Churchill Street.'

'The main one?' Dorothy asked, realising which road he meant.

'Yes. The other members of the committee weren't too happy, but it's a beautiful area to showcase.' He paused as the others agreed.

Abigail continued to explain how the Countdown worked. 'You can post photos any time on the website. There'll be several prizes for the best ones. The leaflet has more information.' Abigail waved to Isabel, the bookshop manager, standing by the counter holding a small white paper in her hand.

Philip stepped forwards, taking one of the leaflets. 'So, you get a stamp or do a QR code? Does it have to be the same every time?'

He looked at Dorothy when he asked this. She wasn't sure why, since she had no idea, but suspected it was because she was the closest. She was glad when someone else replied.

'Yes, that way it can be better tracked,' Oliver answered. 'It's only twelve days, after all.'

'Okay.' Philip flicked through the leaflet. 'Phone feels easier. The details are here, too,' he said, looking at the paper on the shelving unit with the QR code.

'Maybe you and Philip could go to the events together?' Abigail suggested.

Dorothy hesitated, feeling awkward.

Philip seemed to feel the same way, mumbling, 'No, that's not a good idea.'

'How would that work?' Dorothy's voice wavered, unsure.

'I don't think it would be a very good idea,' Philip added. 'I'm better working on my own.'

'Yes, me too. It's a busy time of year, anyway,' Dorothy said, turning towards the door.

'Nonsense! You need a break from that café, Dorothy Wise,' Abigail said, her voice firm.

'I'm taking a break now,' Dorothy retorted, her hand on the door handle.

'We're going to Eagle's Keep tomorrow. We'd love you to come too?' Abigail suggested, referring to the local castle ruins.

Dorothy glared at her friend. 'One hour. Max. Two, if you're lucky. And that depends how busy the café is.'

Abigail smiled, pleased that she had convinced her friend. 'You're already in the bookshop, so you've officially done day one. Although there's an extra bit for this day.' She held Dorothy's gaze and handed her a leaflet. 'You'll know the answer to this question.'

But Dorothy repeated her concern. 'Well, how's that going to work, if he's using his phone and I'm not?' She glared at Abigail, hoping she'd come up with an excuse to step away from the idea.

'You can record the answers separately but discuss them together,' Abigail answered smartly.

Dorothy swallowed. Not what she'd wanted to hear. She looked down at the paper. 'Find a family heirloom in Lavender Village...' she read aloud. 'There must be lots of family heirlooms in the village, but none so famous as your rocking chair.'

Just as she said the words, she felt that strange draft again. As if someone had heard her and was congratulating her.

'Let's not tell anyone else,' Oliver said cheerily, glancing at the clock on the wall. 'There has to be some element of surprise for the rest of the visitors.'

Dorothy managed a smile as she moved towards the shop door. 'Right. Well, I'll see you all later then, shall I?'

'Hang on, what if I can't get to the place on the day?' Philip asked. 'Like, I'm busy or it doesn't interest me?'

'Because you're visiting us, you've got your next twelve days spoken for.' Stephen chuckled. 'But just in case you can't manage to get to the place on the day, then just go anywhere and get a stamp. You won't be penalised if you do that.'

Dorothy was glad to hear that. She'd be able to give out stamps without arguments from her customers. She really should have read the instructions properly.

'The stamps are the same, no matter the place,' Oliver said. 'We've got different events going on to help the business and get more people in on certain days. Now, with all that in mind, we'd better open our doors to our new guests.'

Dorothy smiled and pulled the door open to see a gathering of people waiting to come in. 'Hello,' she said, letting them enter before she stepped out.

'I'll take a photo of the chair,' she heard Philip say.

Not a bad idea, she conceded. But for now, she could write the answer for today's challenge in her booklet and give herself a stamp. She grinned at the time-saving thought.

Chapter Three

D orothy stood by the so-called DIY table making sure the milk containers were full after a complaint from a customer that they were running empty. They'd established the table a while ago to speed up the process of making the customer's drinks. In terms of timing and productivity, it did help.

'Hello, Dorothy!' Abigail called.

'Hello,' Dorothy replied with a smile. It had been a couple of hours since they'd bumped into each other in the bookshop.

'Listen, I've got something I wanted to ask you about,' Abigail said after hugging her friend.

'Okay...' Dorothy hesitated.

'My snow globes have come for my business, and I wanted to ask if you'd like to sell some here.'

Abigail sold household accessories that she often designed herself. Although it was primarily an online store, she always ordered some physical pieces to keep with her. She enjoyed seeing the real thing, and several local businesses stocked her products.

'Oh, that's great!' Dorothy replied. She always wanted to help her friend's business when she could. 'Well, I'd like to have a look at them. Do you have them here with you?'

'Yes.' Abigail nodded, beaming.

'Well, let's see them! I'll meet you over there in a second,' Dorothy said, glancing at the table where, for the first time, she noticed Oliver, Stephen and Philip sat.

A man approached them. He had a noticeable scowl on his face as he demanded, 'Where's the sugar?'

Dorothy sighed inwardly. The worst part of her job was dealing with rude customers. She gestured to the sugar container with a strained smile and turned back towards Abigail.

'There's none left!' the man growled as soon as she turned her back.

'Oh, sorry about that.' She apologised to the man and took the container to the counter, where May and Brian stood. 'Could you fill this, please?' she asked them, setting the container by the cash register.

Having dealt with the customer, Dorothy finally hurried over to her friends' table. Painting a bright smile on her face, she greeted the four of them. 'Hello, everyone. Has someone taken your orders?'

'Yes,' Oliver replied.

'Good.' Dorothy looked around the table and noticed that Philip was watching her intently.

'So, the snow globes,' Abigail announced, pulling a square box from her large, overfilled bag and handing it to Dorothy.

Dorothy gazed at the box which showed Abigail's elegant and sophisticated business logo. 'Can I open it?'

'Yes!' Abigail prompted.

Dorothy opened the box and pulled out a beautiful snow globe with a miniature Lavender Village encased inside. Her own café and the bookshop were included. The colours of a sunset backdropped the scene.

'This is brilliant!' Dorothy held it closer to her face. 'Oh, it even says Rosemary Road!' She pointed to the tiny road sign inside the glass.

'I have another one,' Abigail said, pulling another box from the bag.

Dorothy set the first snow globe on the table and unboxed the second one. 'The rocking chair? That's lovely.' She moved the snow globe from side to side. Inside the globe, the tiny wooden chair rocked as sparkly snow twinkled down upon it. 'It moves! And it's glittery! These are brilliant.'

Abigail grinned. 'I'm glad you like them.'

'I'll take...' Dorothy paused as she calculated. She could put two on each table, but with ten tables, that felt a bit much. Then she considered one of each design by the cash register, but that felt a bit stingy and they might not be seen as much there. That would have been a shame, as they were beautiful products. 'I'll take ten,' she announced eventually. 'Five of each design.'

'You will? Thank you!' Abigail exclaimed. 'I've got eight, including these two. Keep them and I'll bring the rest by later. Dorothy, I'm so grateful. Thank you.'

Dorothy smiled at her friend, then excused herself, seeing she was needed at the cash register.

'Dorothy,' Philip called, moving after her as she crossed the café.

She paused and waited as he approached.

'That was very kind,' Philip said.

'Well, they're beautiful,' Dorothy said. 'And Abigail's very organised. She does most of the work for me; she sets the prices and gives me business cards to display. There's very little for me to do other than find somewhere to display them.'

'You're quite a risk-taker, aren't you?' Philip said with a small smile on his face.

'Um, why?' Dorothy asked, confused. Dorothy wasn't sure why she wanted to hear more of what he had to say, but for some reason she couldn't pull herself away.

'I wonder what you'd be willing to risk...' Philip began, then shook his head. 'Never mind.'

Dorothy stayed quiet, wondering what the heck this guy was on about. To her relief, at that moment Brian came through the swinging kitchen door with a tray full of food.

'Looks like your food's here,' Dorothy said to Philip, relieved to have an excuse to end this strange conversation.

'Yes, it is. I'll see you tomorrow at Eagle's Keep.'

'You'll probably see me in five minutes if I can get to the office for Abigail's money,' Dorothy replied. Living in a place like Lavender Village, it was rare she had a chance to escape to the back of her café without being stopped by several people.

'Of course,' Philip said, returning to the table.

Dorothy tried to understand just what that odd interaction with Philip had been about. Even when they seemed to be having two different conversations, she'd felt a connection like nothing she'd experienced before. As they spoke, her mind had been playing with the idea of what it would be like to hold his hand. Why? She couldn't imagine.

-x-

'I hope you all enjoyed it,' Dorothy said as she hurried over to clear her friends' table once they had finished eating.

'We did, thank you,' Stephen replied.

Dorothy went to pick up the tray, then remembered something. 'Oh, hang on!' She reached into her pocket and took out the cheque, handing it to Abigail. 'I look forward to telling people they're designed by a local businesswoman.'

Abigail took the cheque. 'Thank you so much!'

'Thanks for coming. I really appreciate it,' Dorothy replied, taking the tray and scarpering to the back of the café.

Just as she reached the door to the kitchen, Philip stepped out of the washroom, halting her in her tracks. 'Tomorrow, risk-taker,' he said as he brushed past her.

'Right, yes,' Dorothy replied, still confused.

Dorothy walked into the kitchen, then indicated for May and Brian to come closer. They huddled by the door to the kitchens.

'It seems I've been volunteered to do the Christmas Countdown activities with the Livingstones,' Dorothy told her employees.

'That's great!' May said.

Brian gave a nod. He wasn't much of a talker.

'I may be out attending the events for the next week or so.' Dorothy hesitated on the last few words. Perhaps, she could join in with the first three days and then drop it? Humour her friends a bit. "Now, I know you might want to be involved in it as well, so we'll work around that too.'

She paused as another idea hit her. 'Do you think we need more help in the cafe?'

'I think that's a good idea, especially around Christmas,' May said. 'And if we're going to take part in the Countdown.'

Dorothy appreciated her honesty. 'Right, I'll think about that.'

'Hello?' someone called from the front.

'Right, back to work,' Dorothy said.

Brian turned away, but May hesitated.

'Everything okay?' Dorothy asked.

'That guy you were speaking with...' May began. 'He's got the hots for you.'

Dorothy shook her head, dismissing the idea. 'May, it's time to work.'

Her employee sighed. 'Okay, okay...'

Dorothy walked to the dishwasher and set the tray down more heartily than intended. *Did* he have the hots for her? Is that what his weird behaviour was about?

Ridiculous nonsense, she decided as she unloaded the tray and moved towards the counter, beginning to ice the cakes.

Chapter Four

♥

Countdown Day 2

Eleven days until Christmas

'Will you be alright?' Dorothy asked May, her face contorted with anxiety from a mixture of leaving the café during the busy Christmas period and a reluctance to do this activity.

'We'll be fine.'

Not the reply she wanted to hear.

'How are we doing with Abigail's snow globes?' Dorothy asked.

'They're on the tables, and they have her details on the bottom. I've left a few of her cards out as well,' Brian replied.

'Okay.' Dorothy felt better at hearing this. 'Right, well, I'll be back in a couple of hours or so...'

'Bye!' May said assuredly.

Her employee's firm tone jarred Dorothy into action, and she moved towards the door.

-x-

'Hello, everyone,' Dorothy said as she approached the waiting group gathered outside her café. They had all planned to walk to the castle together.

Many replied with waves and smiles. Lots of couples, she noticed, looking at Abigail with her arm wrapped around Stephen, Cameron and Isabel holding hands and a new couple who she wasn't familiar with.

The whole thing reminded her of a *Bridget Jones* movie. Everyone seemed to be married or with someone. Except her.

And Philip.

Cameron stepped forwards, gesturing to the couple standing next to him. 'Dorothy, this is my brother, Angus.' A younger version of Cameron waved to her. 'And this is Sophie, his girlfriend.'

An excited-looking girl in her early twenties stepped forwards, her red curls bouncing. 'Hi!'

'Right, shall we begin?' Cameron asked. 'As your self-delegated tour guide—'

'We're not even over the bridge and he's already preaching at us,' Angus complained loudly, and several people chuckled.

This didn't stop Cameron. 'I will be your tour guide today,' he repeated to the soundtrack of Angus' audible sigh. 'For those of you who don't know, I work at Eagle's Keep, and although I'm not in uniform, I am familiar with the topic and the building. I have written and prepared some of the displays there.'

Cameron continued speaking as they walked down the road in the direction of the bridge. 'Eagle's Keep was a castle ruin which has been redone and now demonstrates the history of the area. It has taken many years and several legends to create the new Eagle's Keep Historical Site.'

Dorothy smiled. She enjoyed Cameron's enthusiasm.

'I, myself, have contributed to the death rituals and many of the cultural points.' He stopped to be sure everyone was together. 'Come on, Angus, would you?'

His brother glared at him, but moved as directed.

The group followed as Cameron occasionally stopped to give facts about the history of the castle. Dorothy chatted with Abigail, but became distracted when she sensed Philip walking close behind them.

They reached the other side of the bridge, where the ticket booth was located, and paused while Cameron addressed the group again.

Philip stepped closer to Dorothy, whispering, 'How are you today?'

'I'm well, thanks. And you?' Dorothy felt an unfamiliar dose of nerves. She put it down to this new experience with a group of people.

'I'm very well.' Philip stopped to let her go first as they reached the ticket booth.

'Christmas Countdown papers, please!' Cameron called. He took this job very seriously. 'I'll meet you over there.' Cameron pointed to an area where the grass met a path.

Dorothy gave a nod. She could manage that. She stepped in Philip's direction as he prepared to QR scan his phone. Those who had the Christmas Countdown booklets pulled out their papers, ready to get them stamped.

'Does anyone call you Dot?' Philip asked suddenly.

'No. Why?'

'Just wondered.'

Odd, Dorothy thought as she moved over to the meeting place. But she couldn't help but notice he smelled like coffee and a woodsy aftershave. She liked it.

Once they had all gathered again, Cameron continued, 'Eagle's Keep is actually a ruined castle, but the council has made it into a historical location. You can go inside and see pictures and artefacts, reflecting how it would have looked throughout history. They have jousting, Victorian-style rooms, medieval costumes and signage that reminds us of Britain's history.'

Everyone looked up at the wooden post Cameron pointed to, which had several markers pointing in various directions. They showed the names of other British historical sites including the Round Table, the White Cliffs of Dover, the New Forest and more.

It was Sophie who stared at it the longest. 'That doesn't make sense,' she said, looking at the group. 'It's wrong. Stonehenge is further that way, not this direction. It's more to the left than the right.'

Her words were met with a flash of silence, but Cameron took it all in his stride. 'So, if you were designing a map, you'd point it in that direction, rather than the way it is?'

'But I'm not designing a map. I'm looking at it here. The roads might go in that direction, but it doesn't mean they don't move up eventually. It doesn't feel right,' Sophie said, earning a cuddle from her boyfriend.

'Sophie's right,' Philip piped up.

Everybody turned to look at him, and Dorothy's eyes widened.

'It *is* in the wrong direction. If you're going by road, everything should go back that way, over the bridge. But they don't. That doesn't make sense,' he explained.

'It's meant to show the general direction,' someone said. Dorothy wasn't sure who.

Dorothy was sure she'd never heard so much discussion around a sign in her life. She almost wanted to stop the conversation and tell them all to keep moving. This just felt silly.

'And the number is wrong,' Philip added.

'The number is wrong?' Cameron asked with a chuckle.

'Yep. It is written in paces, rather than miles, but if you convert it, it's saying there are around seventy miles between here and Stonehenge, but that's not true. It's more like fifty or sixty miles to Stonehenge from here. Seventy miles would reach Oxford,' Philip stated. 'Did you have anything to do with it?'

'Sorry?' Cameron almost choked on the word.

'This sign,' Philip said matter-of-factly. 'Did you have anything to do with the making of this sign?'

'No,' Cameron replied, flustered. He quickly recovered. 'I contributed to the death rituals,' he added, emphasising the word *death*.

The comment earned laughter from the group. Dorothy bit her lip, believing Philip to be obnoxious for starting such a conversation, especially since he was new to the group.

'Well, look, these are paces, right?' Philip asked Cameron. Dorothy realised he wasn't trying to be difficult, he just seemed to be quite strongly opinionated. 'Roman paces.'

'Yep,' Cameron replied confidently, back on form after his earlier challenge.

'Right, so we have seventy miles, which, if we walked, would be one thousand paces per mile. Seventy thousand paces,' Philip explained. 'From Stonehenge, seventy thousand paces in our direction would take you to Oxford, which is further north than us. We're closer than that. If we calculated it based on Roman paces, we'd be around fifty-eight thousand paces from Stonehenge.'

No one said a word. They just absorbed Philp's announcement. Dorothy raised an eyebrow as she processed his comments. He had shown confidence amongst this group, and he was clearly very logical. That was attractive to her.

'Very good,' Cameron managed. 'Well, that was a very detailed explanation. Thank you, Philip.'

A few murmurs of thanks and acknowledgement rang around, but most people looked on in a mixture of confusion and awe.

'There is a box for feedback, if you wanted to add anything about that,' Cameron offered.

Dorothy hoped Philip didn't. She imagined the rest of the numbers weren't accurate either, given the numbers all ended in zeros. But to correct it felt a bit pernickety.

Cameron continued the tour as the group walked across the grass, stating, 'Now please follow me to the right. Careful where you walk there's a—'

A squeal escaped Dorothy as she attempted to keep her balance on the uneven ground. A hand shot out to steady her, and she took it, giving an appreciative glance towards the person, who just happened to be Philip.

'—dip,' Cameron finished, just as Philip pulled her to safety.

'Cameron!' Angus cursed. 'You should have warned us sooner.'

'Sorry, Dorothy. Are you alright?' Cameron asked sincerely.

'I'll be okay,' she replied. She moved her arm to hint to Philip that he could release it. He had held it a little longer than necessary, but Dorothy quietly appreciated his concern.

'My brother likes to joke around.' Angus said, still glaring at Cameron. 'There's a dip in the ground by the flower bed. He finds it funny.'

Dorothy felt silly for not seeing the obvious dip. She promised herself she would be more careful and aware of where she was walking from now on.

Philip released her hand, but he stayed by her side. A protective gesture which she didn't complain about.

They chatted as they followed the group, and Dorothy learned that Philip had an interest in jousting and that Eagle's Keep had a jousting society. He seemed keen to discover more about it.

The fact that he liked such a sport made her intrigued. 'You think I'm the risk-taker? Doing something like that would be even braver,' she said, surprised by her own confidence.

That made him smile, but before he could say anything else, they reached the castle and Cameron took their attention again.

The renovated castle was interesting, filled with all sorts of information and items ranging from medieval to Victorian times, and even some more modern things.

Dorothy found it to be a most interesting place. She was glad the council had decided to do this. Not only was it restoring an important historical place, but it also lent a new landmark to their village. She vowed to return sometime next year.

The group paused by a set of old photographs of the building as Cameron told them stories and legends that she'd had no idea about.

'Bank robbers hid here for three days before the police arrived,' he explained. 'Yes, I know it seems ridiculous. It's a cliff, so where else could they go, right? But the plan went wrong. They threw the treasure down there.' He pointed to the picture of the cliff and the artist's image of the old castle. 'The boat wasn't there, and it all fell in the water. The authorities didn't know...'

As Cameron continued the tale, Dorothy looked around. She saw Philip with a stoic expression on his face and wondered what he was thinking about. He stood only a few feet away from her, just as he had for the whole visit. She appreciated that. Although she could have managed the fall on her own, she was glad he was there to help her.

After the tour concluded, the group trailed out of the building. Leaving the castle almost felt like shaking off a spell and entering a different reality so dissimilar to the world they had been in.

'That was fun,' Dorothy said to Philip, who was still walking closely beside her. 'I'm so glad I did that.'

Philip smiled in return.

As the group headed over the bridge, Dorothy turned to them. 'Anyone want a cup of tea, since we're so close to the café?'

They all declined, Christmas shopping and other pressing priorities among the reasons.

Dorothy smiled. 'Okay, maybe another time. Catch you later! And thank you, Cameron.'

Once back in her office, reminiscing on the day with a cup of tea and cake, Dorothy decided that Philip wasn't as bad as she'd initially thought. But she wasn't in a hurry to let anyone know that just yet.

Chapter Five

♥

Countdown Day 3

Ten days until Christmas

Walking out of the kitchen, Dorothy was glad to see her friends sitting at a table in her café. Her gaze took in the gang: Abigail and Stephen, Isabel and Cameron, Angus and Sophie, and even Oliver. Her smile widened even more as she saw Philip look up from his phone. Waves of happiness and gratitude rushed over her at seeing them all there.

'How is everyone today?' she welcomed them.

'Great, thank you!' Abigail said, and the others responded similarly.

'Right, so today we have the Festive Special.' Dorothy lifted one of the plastic-wrapped mugs bulging with treats. 'It includes an orange biscuit and two gingerbread people with a choice of hot chocolate, coffee or tea.'

She beamed at the group, who all smiled back. She watched one smile in particular: Philip's. The ends of his mouth curled upwards and the blue in his eyes deepened.

In an effort to refocus, Dorothy added, 'So what would everybody like to drink?'

They all reeled off their orders and Dorothy confirmed, 'Okay, so four teas, three coffees and one hot chocolate. I'll get things started.'

'Wait, Dorothy,' Abigail said before she could leave. 'What are orange biscuits?'

Dorothy paused. She thought about the biscuits in the oven and Brian in charge of them. 'When I come back, it'll make more sense.'

-x-

The conversation was bright and lively when she returned. Philip was telling Oliver how he used to ride horses at Christmas. It had started with donkeys, but they were boring, apparently. Then, he had volunteered in the stables and they let him ride. That was what got him into jousting.

Dorothy smiled as she placed teapots and cups on the table and the end of the song "Little Donkey" played through the café's speaker system.

'So, tell everyone about the biscuit competition earlier this year,' Abigail said, getting the attention of the entire table.

Dorothy glanced around, making sure the other customers didn't need her attention. 'You can tell it. Or Isabel. You were both there.'

'It's not the same,' Abigail said quickly.

'Okay...' Dorothy relented. 'Last spring I had a biscuit competition here, at the shop. We had the press and cameras so everyone could see in the back, and we had three youths come in to try out their skills. We had the mayor and three judges: Abigail and Isabel were two of them.' She nodded to her friends. 'And a third one. Can't remember his name.'

Abigail waved a hand to hurry her along.

'Anyway, the kids cooked and the judges tried the food and voted. And Peyton Miles won. He cooked his grandmother's orange biscuit recipe, which is what you've got here.' She gestured to the biscuits the group was eating. 'He's gone to culinary school since, but he'll be stopping by today.'

'They're delicious,' Philip said, swallowing a mouthful.

'They are, aren't they?' Dorothy agreed.

The group splintered into several different conversations, and Philip leaned in to Dorothy. 'My mum used to cook with me and my younger sister Connie at Christmas. It was the only time she did that. It was always fun.'

'I didn't know you had a sister. How much younger is she?' Dorothy asked, realising how odd it was that she knew almost nothing about him.

'Two years,' he replied. 'Do you have any siblings?'

'No, I'm an only child.'

'What's your favourite Christmas song?' he asked, changing the subject.

'"Oh, Come All Ye Faithful,"' Dorothy said. 'That and "Hark the Herald," sung by a really good choir.'

Philip smiled at her response. Suddenly, a memory of a small cottage with a pink door popped into her head. She couldn't put her finger on why she'd thought about it and wondered about its significance.

'Sorry,' she said, blinking away the memory. 'Does it often snow in Manchester?' she asked, now forgetting about the other customers and pulling over a seat to sit at the table. 'I always imagined it like that James Herriot show.'

'I live about eight miles from the centre of Manchester,' Philip said. 'And, yeah, we get snow. My dad used to take us sledding.' He turned to Oliver to include him in the conversation. 'Mum, not so much. She stayed in to read a book or something. Where are you from?'

'Cornwall. The west side,' Dorothy said. 'Didn't snow much. Bad storms, though.'

The conversation moved on, with Oliver interjecting his own stories, and Dorothy sat back and smiled as she watched her friends talking. A veil of happiness floated over her.

Suddenly the shrill shriek of a chair scraping against the floor drew her attention.

'I've got to leave for work,' Sophie said. 'But thanks, this was fun!'

'Did you get a stamp?' Dorothy shot out of her seat and hurried to the counter to get the stamps for the booklets. She stamped Sophie's first before the rest of the gang's papers.

In the rushed thanks and goodbyes, Dorothy felt an overwhelming sense of contentment. The arms of friendship had hugged her, and she had got to know Philip a little better.

Chapter Six

♥

Countdown Day 4

Nine days until Christmas

Dorothy entered the community centre and looked around for a table to place the large box she was carrying. It was full of extra Festive Special mugs which she wanted to donate. She had kept some back to sell, but she wanted to share the rest with the community.

Suddenly, someone put a hand underneath the box she held. 'Looks like it's about to break!' Stephen warned.

'Oh, thank you,' Dorothy said as they shuffled together towards a table. It was rather intimate, but she knew Stephen well enough not to feel awkward.

'I was just bringing over some of Abigail's snow globes,' Stephen explained, the box now safely on the surface.

'They've sold really well in the café,' Dorothy said. 'I was going to ask for more.'

'That's great! I'll let her know,' Stephen replied, nodding politely to a grumpy-looking lady in a Christmas jumper on the other side of the table.

'You do know we can't sell them? Nothing here is for sale; it's all donation,' the woman said, her sharp words landing like bullets.

Dorothy was aware of this and didn't need such a harsh reminder. It was Christmastime, after all. 'It's a donation,' she said, pushing the box towards the lady. She had put business cards on all the packages so people could find her.

'Hmm. Thank you,' the lady said in dismissal.

Dorothy felt a sense of satisfaction at having donated the mugs, but part of her wondered if it had been the right choice. She was running a business, after all. She tried not to think about all the money lost and instead focussed on how good it felt to help out her community. Plus, she'd had the café long enough that it was making a profit. Worrying was a natural human thing, she decided.

'Do you want to join us?' Stephen asked, breaking Dorothy from her thoughts. He was pointing to a large table with all her friends seated around it.

'Everyone's here?' she asked, surprised. She had been so wrapped up in her thoughts that somehow she hadn't noticed.

'It is a large group tonight. Dad was going to come but he felt it was going to be too rowdy.'

Dorothy thought about Oliver, probably happy and eating his supper at home, and gave Stephen a compassionate smile.

'Hello, Dorothy!' Abigail announced cheerily as she and Stephen approached the table. She got up from her seat and hugged her friend.

Dorothy reciprocated the hug. It was strange that after all these years of friendship she still felt grateful for being accepted by Abigail.

'Hi,' Dorothy waved to everyone, noting the faces. Sophie, Angus, Isabel, Cameron and Philip.

They all waved back and she sat down in the empty seat, Philip to her right and Stephen to her left.

'Hi, Philip. How are you?' she asked politely.

'Good,' came the reply. He had a slight smile on his face. 'We're going to play a board game. We all voted and chose Trivial Pursuit.'

Not her favourite, but Dorothy kept smiling anyway, not wanting to seem difficult.

'It looks like it's you and me as partners,' Philip said, and she felt he was watching her reaction a little more carefully than would be typical.

'Okay.' Dorothy looked to the middle of the table where the game was set up. She wanted to glance at Abigail, figuring this pairs situation had worked out with her input. 'We're green?'

Philip gave a nod. 'I'm best at History, Science and Sports.'

'Good, you can take care of those.' Dorothy prayed that whatever her strong points were, they be found quickly. 'Did you vote for this?'

'Yeah, it's one of my favourites.'

Just then, a voice announced to the hall: 'Welcome, ladies, gentlemen and youngsters.'

She turned to see who was speaking. A tall, stringy man in a green Christmas jumper stood at the end of the hall, clutching a microphone.

'My name is Max Evans. Tonight's game night is part of the Christmas Countdown celebration. We are glad for your support!'

Max paused while the crowd applauded.

'We have pamphlets on the other services we run.' Max held a glossy flyer up in his hand. 'And we see tonight as a chance to get to know each other, support the village and show what we do in the community.

Don't forget your Christmas Countdown stamps. Either come to myself or Lillian to get one.'

He pointed to the woman who had taken Dorothy's box. Lilian nodded as a mass of faces obediently turned in her direction. She responded with a fierce look which Dorothy thought could be interpreted as a smile.

Max continued, gesturing around the room as he said, 'The QR code is taped to the tables and on the walls at various points around the space.'

Dorothy almost wanted to laugh as she watched the man going to the effort of pointing the pictures out. He reminded her of someone, though she couldn't pinpoint who. A tall, gangly man...

Max continued to talk, but Dorothy zoned out. Then she felt something bump against her leg. She froze, trying to figure out what it was, but it moved away before she could.

Must've been her imagination.

Finally, the game began. Dorothy was tired from the introduction speech and for the first few moves she had to focus extra hard on the rules and questions of the game. But, to her delight, she could answer the questions without trouble and their green piece moved around the board quicker than most of the others.

At one point, Philip accidentally knocked Isabel and Cameron's pieces off the board as he moved theirs.

'Sorry,' he said, bending down to pick them up. 'Where are they?' he asked, rubbing a hand on Dorothy's leg under the table.

She laughed and looked down with a smile. He greeted her with a grinning face and two of the coloured slices in his hand. They were still missing one, but he quickly found it, just by her boot on the tiled floor.

'What are you two doing?' someone asked, and another laugh brought Dorothy up to face the players.

'We were looking for the—'

Philip held the green wedge in his hand. 'There were only three, right?'

'Three, yes. Thank you.' Cameron sounded annoyed.

Dorothy hurriedly placed the part on the board. 'Whose turn was it?' she asked.

'Yours,' Angus said with a slight smirk. 'I'll get ready to ask a question.'

It turned out that question won the last wedge and an extra roll. All they had to do now was move up the line to the central hub. It was a battle, as Abigail and Stephen were just ahead of them.

Two dice shakes later, just one space behind Abigail and Stephen's, Philip confidently answered a Sports and Leisure question. The dice roll allowed them to take the lead and they both cheered. Then Dorothy felt something on her thigh, and she knew it was Philip's hand. A warm feeling trickled through her.

On the next move, Abigail and Stephen moved into the centre. They had won.

Dorothy prepared to answer the next question, and luckily she knew the answer: 'Pepper and mustard,' she said, much to Cameron's dismay.

'How do you know that?' Cameron asked.

'Cooking facts stick with me,' Dorothy said, her gaze moving to Philip.

'We came second!' Philip punched the air.

'Shush,' Dorothy scolded him jokily.

'I know, but...' Philip stood and took her hand, pulling her from the chair.

'What are you doing?'

'Dancing,' Philip said, swinging her around.

She rolled her eyes. 'We didn't win.'

'No, we came in second.' They danced for a couple of seconds, then he suggested, 'Let's get some popcorn for everyone.'

'Yes, and some of those Festive Specials that you brought!' Cameron exclaimed.

There was only one Festive Special mug left. Dorothy picked it up, and by the time they returned to the table, the others had packed up the board game.

'We decided that was enough for us,' Isabel said. 'We're thinking Snap or something less taxing on the brain. Anyone want to play?'

There were no takers.

'It's nine o'clock,' Dorothy said. 'I have to go soon.' She put the popcorn on the table and set the mug next to Cameron, who thanked her gleefully. 'It's the last one.'

Philip put his hand on the back of the empty chair next to him, indicating for her to sit down, which she did.

'So, aside from knowing lots about cooking, what made you open the café?' he asked.

Dorothy hadn't realised just how significant this question was to her. 'I've always wanted to run one. I used to make biscuits and meringues with Mum when I was little. Got rather good at it. I loved bringing food to school. Contrary to my friends' belief, I wasn't sucking up. I just loved cooking and sharing.'

'Where's your mum now?' Philip asked. 'You don't mention her.'

'She died,' Dorothy confessed. 'Twelve years ago. Both of my parents died in a plane crash. I came here after that.' The hurt still pierced her. 'I went to culinary school and learned the basics and some advanced stuff too.'

'I'm sorry to hear about your parents,' Philip said. 'But I think it's very impressive that you run your own business. You're clearly very talented.'

Dorothy smiled. 'What about you? How come you know so much about business?' she asked, having noticed that he seemed to talk about the topic a lot when in group situations.

'I'm a business strategist,' Philip said. 'I advise large companies how to run their business, what to do next ... stuff like that. Half of them don't know how their businesses got so big, while the others don't do what you say, despite hiring me for advice. Bunch of nonsense, really.'

Dorothy sat quietly for a moment. 'You don't enjoy it? You're here for a break, right? Do you want to go back?'

Philip's eyes darkened. 'I'm not going back there after Christmas. I'll be finding another job. They...' He trailed off, shaking his head. 'I won't go back there.'

'Okay.' Dorothy paused. 'But would you want to go back into that general line of work?'

'Yeah, I want to stay in the industry,' Philip said.

Dorothy realised she'd hit a nerve, so she changed the subject. 'Your family's in Manchester, right?'

Philip stiffened. Oh dear, she'd hit another nerve.

'Mum and my sister,' he said, then paused. 'My dad's buried there, too. It was rather sudden. Bit of a long story.' He looked back at her, then glanced around the room to where several other couples were now dancing. 'Sure you don't want to dance?'

Dorothy's face burst into a smile, then she sighed good-naturedly. 'Okay then, if we can find a quieter spot.'

He stood and took her hand, leading her to a quieter area.

'"Jingle Bell Rock,"' he announced, setting a hand on her waist. 'This is my favourite Christmas song.'

As they moved, Dorothy remembered the odd feeling she'd had when the cottage had popped into her mind. It was the last place she and her parents had stayed before their deaths.

She pressed herself closer to Philip, relishing the comfort of another human's touch.

Chapter Seven

♥

Countdown Day 5

Eight days until Christmas

I t was two o'clock in the afternoon and Dorothy had left the shop in May's capable hands as she was back at the community centre. Once again, Max Evans stood with the microphone, addressing the crowd.

Suddenly, Dorothy realised what was so familiar about him. 'He looks like John Cleese,' she muttered from where they stood around the perimeter of the room.

This earnt a smile from Abigail. 'I know, it's the height, isn't it?' she whispered back.

Again, Dorothy missed much of what Max was saying. She looked at the two long rows of tables and her inner child came out. Pieces of card, felt tips and assorted craft stuff lay on the tables. And Dorothy wanted to create.

Max (aka. John Cleese) was babbling. He had to mention the supporters and sponsors. And the school. The school which had turned up and...

Abigail discreetly moved over to the tables full of crafts and grabbed a piece of card, then walked back to where Dorothy was standing.

Children fidgeted. A few adults hushed them.

Dorothy's gaze wandered to the craft tables, her eye catching on the glittery pieces that lay scattered on it. Slowly, she shuffled towards the tables, just as John Cleese explained why they were making the cards.

'Can't they start?' a voice whispered. 'I can't keep them hanging on for much longer. It's like a Spanish bull chase.'

Dorothy wanted to laugh, but John Cleese kept talking: 'When you have made your cards, we ask you not to address them. Sign your names if you wish. But...'

'Can they start now?' the same desperate voice asked, louder this time. Dorothy turned to see a young woman holding a child's hand as if in restraint.

'Well, yes, I suppose they can,' John Cleese answered, as if taken aback.

A moment later, a cheer arose and loud chatter erupted in the air as children found their seats and began crafting Christmas cards.

'These cards will be donated to the hospital for the children who...' Although John Cleese's volume increased, no one was listening.

Dorothy, for her part, didn't care where the cards were going. It wasn't to be rude; she just wanted the joy of creating a card.

She joined a table with her friends and reached for a piece of purple paper. She wasn't sure why as it wasn't even a colour she particularly liked, but something about it caught her attention.

After making her first card, Dorothy sat back and observed her friends. Philip and Stephen sat opposite her and Abigail. It was just the four of them today. Stephen was shading a night sky in pencil. It was simple yet effective. Philip had turned to the side and was digging through what looked like a laptop bag.

'I like that the stamps can be used anywhere,' Dorothy said. 'Although, I like the idea of having a more specialised stamp for the Countdown with my logo or something. But I'm not arguing with customers or saying we can't stamp their thing because it's the wrong day.'

'Dad said the committee considered that,' Stephen looked up from his picture. 'But with so many businesses he was all for simplicity. He said you'd lose the point if the stamps were too pretty or fiddly with exact dates. Besides, they had to get them done in time for Christmas and it would have been more expensive to personalise them all. They just wanted Christmas marketing to happen, not to get lost in the details.' Carefully, Stephen brushed his picture to fade the pencil shading. 'He wanted the community to get to know each other and for business to increase. Have you noticed a difference in the numbers these last few days, Dorothy?'

'Well, we've certainly been busy. I must admit, I'm glad to have my employees. I've tried to encourage them to come to the events, too. I think it's only fair. That said, I'd rather have them at the shop,' she confessed. 'We've been really busy since we've been selling the Festive Specials. I guess with us making the food *and* selling it, we need all hands on deck.'

Abigail smiled at her friend, 'I'm glad you're doing the activities. You're going to come to more of them, right?'

'I'll think about it...' Dorothy said with a chuckle.

-x-

'Are you going back to the café?' Philip asked as they left the community centre forty minutes later.

'Yes,' Dorothy said, looking at the three friends to see if they wanted to join her.

'Mind if I—' Philip began.

'Well, I've got to check on Dad,' Stephen interrupted, forging ahead.

'I've got to get home too,' Abigail said. 'Got some business matters to attend to... Stephen! Hold on,' she called, hurrying to her partner.

Dorothy almost smiled at her friends' reactions, until she questioned why they were acting so strangely. Did she and Philip seem so close that Abigail would feel like a gooseberry if left alone with them?

She shrugged it off and turned towards the café, walking alongside Philip.

'So, what do you do as a business strategist?' she asked Philip. Their shoulders bumped slightly as they moved.

'Well, we set mission and value statements. See where the company is headed and develop a plan to incorporate them.'

'Oh, right.' Dorothy felt his arm wrap around her and smiled. She felt more and more comfortable talking to him every time they had a conversation. 'Could you do it for any business?' she asked, looking up at him.

Philip cocked an eyebrow. 'Well, I suppose we could apply the principles to any business. Why?'

'Well...' Dorothy paused. 'You help companies expand, right?'

'Diversify is the broader term.' Now both eyebrows arched. 'What are you thinking?'

Dorothy wasn't sure what she was thinking, but continued, 'Let's take my business, for example. Without getting too personal or into the specifics, what do you think would help me increase my profits?'

Philip stopped, turning to Dorothy. 'That's a loaded question. What's your long-term aim?' He squeezed his arms around her, and she felt a warmth surround her. 'I'm presuming you have some long-term goals? You've been in business for twelve years, right? And you're pulling a profit?'

'Yes, that's not quite my concern,' Dorothy replied, distracted by the scent of mint from his breath in the cold air.

'Do you have some long-term plans, maybe for more employees? Or to retire? Work less?' He released his arms and disappointment visited her. 'I can identify any mistakes you have made or any big risks you have taken and offer suggestions on how to help.'

'Okay.'

'Have you?' Philip asked, biting his lip.

'What?' She was distracted. 'Sorry.'

'Taken any big risks?'

'Oh, well...' she stuttered.

What's with the risk-taking? she wondered. Despite feeling more comfortable around him, Dorothy felt like this question held a sense of judgement. Having been in business for so long, perhaps she should have more to show for it. After all, the biggest risk she'd taken in a while was adding orange biscuits to the menu.

Perhaps it was time to review things.

'Does it make more sense now? My work, I mean?' Philip asked, watching her.

'Uh, well ... not really.' She still needed clarification or a more specific examination of her own business.

They had arrived at the corner of Rosemary Road, where her café was situated. Ready to take the attention off herself, Dorothy pushed open the café door and entered the shop.

Something wasn't right. May stood in the dining area talking to a man, and their voices were raised.

Dorothy turned to Philip. 'Find a seat,' she advised. 'I'm just going to—'

'Are you the boss of this establishment?' the man who had been talking to May interrupted.

Oh, here we go, another complainer, Dorothy thought, but forced a smile onto her face.

'I am.'

'My son doesn't like orange biscuits!'

Dorothy waited. Out of the corner of her eye, she noticed May scurrying back to the kitchen, glad to get away from the angry man.

'That girl just told me you have gingerbread men or Victoria sponge, but nothing else.'

Dorothy's back bristled. May was not a "girl".

'If that's all we have left, then that's all we have for today,' she answered.

A sudden fresh sensation visited her. Normally, when a customer got angry, she stayed quiet and let them speak. But today, with the echo of the word *risk-taker* in the back of her mind, she decided not to do that.

'What sort of café is this?' the man demanded. His oval face scowled as he loomed over Dorothy.

Dorothy wasn't sure how she did it, but she straightened her spine and answered, 'One that is about to close and is offering a limited supply of very tasty baked foods.'

The café fell into silence. Even the man stayed quiet for a beat.

'Now, I am sorry that we can't acknowledge your son's needs at the moment. But I'm sure if he comes in tomorrow afternoon, we'll have something different available.'

The man glared at her. 'What did you just say? Are you being rude and mocking my—'

'No.' Dorothy found herself looking up at the man's face. She couldn't let him intimidate her. *Risk-taker, risk-taker*, she thought. 'I'm saying that tomorrow we'll have some other foods on the menu. Right now, we don't. What does your son like?'

'What?' the man eased off, clearly taken aback.

'Is there a particular food that your son likes to eat?' Dorothy asked. 'We could make that for him for tomorrow.'

The man gaped. It seemed he either hadn't thought of this solution or didn't know how to respond to it.

'Meringue snowmen!' a young voice said.

Dorothy looked down to see a child at her waist. 'Meringues?'

The boy nodded.

'Alright, I'll make some meringue snowmen. But you'd better come quickly tomorrow, or they might be all gone.'

'Hmmph,' the man grumbled. He reached for his child, who escaped his grasp.

'Meringue snowmen tomorrow,' Dorothy reiterated. 'I won't be saving any, though. They go quickly.'

'Johnnie!' the man said. He turned to the boy and Dorothy followed his gaze.

Dear heavens! Now the child was standing on a chair, doing a strange dance.

The father stomped over to him, but thankfully Philip reached the boy before he fell from the chair, bending slightly to be eye level with the child. He said a few words to him. Dorothy did not know what was exchanged, but the child clambered down before the father reached him.

In utter silence, the pair left.

Dorothy exhaled a long sigh as Philip moved over to her. On other occasions, she'd offer the remaining customers free drinks or biscuits.

But right now, she simply stood, fighting between exhaustion and the strength to pick up and start again. With words lost in her head, she sat down on the nearest chair.

'We apologise,' Philip said to the other patrons. 'Please, continue with your day.'

With the rest of the café gradually returning to their own conversations, Philip sat down next to Dorothy. 'Hey,' he said. 'I think you handled that very well.'

'Thank you.' Dorothy touched his hand, giving him a weary smile.

Chapter Eight

♥

As it turned out, Philip decided to spend the entire afternoon with her in the café. He reassured her and even assisted her in bringing food over to customers and chatting to them.

Finally, at closing, Dorothy asked where he was eating supper, which he admitted he hadn't considered.

'Then you're coming with me,' she announced, feeling confident and grateful. It was the least she could do as a thank you.

Philip smiled. He didn't turn down the offer, as she feared. Instead, he put an arm around her lower back as she locked the café door.

As they set off, Dorothy remembered the night she first learned of Philip, when she was locking the door and a rough voice was talking to Oliver through a car window.

And here he was now.

She cuddled into him.

'So, what are you planning for supper?' Philip asked in a low voice.

For a moment, Dorothy forgot the menu. She took in his caffeine-induced scent from the coffee he'd drank in the café. A hint of musk floated by her nose, too.

'Pasta and cheese.' The second word was issued with some hesitation. 'Do you eat cheese?'

'I do,' he replied.

Dorothy poked her head from under his arm. 'Something is going on with the sky. The moon is brighter than usual.'

His stoic expression became more serious. 'A sign of snow.'

Dorothy relaxed into him. 'Thank you for helping me today and staying this afternoon. It was very kind.'

She felt him smile and his arm tightened around her.

'I don't think you have my mobile phone number, do you?' she asked. 'When we get to my house I'll give it to you.' It seemed an odd request, given how close they had become, but it seemed a sensible step, too.

'When we get inside,' Philip said, his voice gravelly. He looked at the row of houses to their left. 'Which one is it?'

'Oh, just around the corner.' She was sure the last word got swallowed up in a whisper. 'Mulberry Lane, the second one in.'

They continued their walk and Dorothy felt warm emotions shoot around her body. Part of her wanted to stay outside. She enjoyed the warmth he gave her.

'What's on the Countdown calendar for tomorrow?' Philip asked.

'The community centre is open for crafts. Something about building snowmen. I think they're going to have foam and crafty stuff. Or maybe big pieces you can have your picture taken with...' She swallowed and trailed off awkwardly.

They paused walking. Philip shifted, his face appearing in front of hers, bright eyes meeting her gaze. 'Will you be going?' he asked.

'I don't know.' She felt she was dancing on coals. 'I've seen enough of Mr Cleese for a while.'

A laugh barrelled out of him. 'I think we're here.' He pointed to her house.

'Oh, yes.'

How had that happened? Suddenly, Dorothy was feeling all jelly-like inside. She wasn't thinking about supper, but more about how quickly they could get their coats off.

She walked up the steps and he loosened his grip around her as she opened her bag to find her key.

'In your pocket,' Philip offered.

'Oh.' An embarrassed smile changed into one of relief when she pulled the keys from her pocket. She couldn't remember putting them there!

He waited for her to enter first and followed her. Just as the door closed, he turned around and gently backed her against it. His face lowered until it was just inches from hers. 'May I kiss you, Dorothy?'

As he waited for her response, she whipped off her gloves. They landed somewhere on the floor. Then she pulled his face to hers and they kissed softly.

They parted and Philip swallowed, his Adam's apple bobbing. 'I've been wanting to do that for ages.'

'Since when?' Dorothy asked.

'Since the castle,' Philip managed.

Dorothy wasn't sure whether to laugh or gasp in disbelief. He hadn't really shown any interest in her then!

This thought was ripped away when he reached for the zip on her coat and said, 'Let's get this off.'

'You're my guest; we have to take yours off, too.'

'Be rude not to,' Philip agreed, now peeling off her sweater.

'Hang on,' Dorothy said, though she didn't want to stop. 'The odds aren't even. You're taking more off than...'

She lost the words as his hand cupped her bottom. Heat ran through her. She wondered if people of her age – in her forties – should do such things! Shouldn't she have left that behind by now?

She tried to remember how old Philip was. Did she know? Did it matter?

'Sit down,' he growled, leading her to a chair by the front door.

She did as he asked, eagerly awaiting the next command.

'I'm taking your boots off.' His fingers ran up her legs as they undid the zips.

Dorothy was sure she'd never felt anything like this in her life. Never. Not in her teenage years, twenties or any other time.

As this tall, powerful man undressed her, he didn't seem to mind if she was a little pudgy in places and he delighted in running his hands over her thighs. He made her feel delicious.

She wasn't entirely sure when it was going to stop, but she realised it didn't really matter. She held his gaze as he knelt next to her on the tiled floor, cupped her chin and gave her a long, deep kiss.

Eventually, Dorothy moved her head back a little and said, 'Fun as this is, I think we better get some food.'

Flushed, Philip smiled and ran his hands from her thighs to land on her waist. 'Food? That sounds rather good.'

'I don't want to spoil the moment...' Dorothy said.

'You aren't,' he replied.

'Come and help me cook. The carrots n-need to be chopped,' she stammered.

Philip pulled her up into a standing position and she blushed when she realised she was now only wearing her underwear. She was glad she had put on her deep red and lacey underwear set this morning. The ones she usually left until she'd done all her laundry.

Chapter Nine

♥

They entered the kitchen and Philip grabbed a long, floral, cream-coloured apron that was hanging on the side of the fridge. 'You're cooking,' he said as he placed it over her head, then reached around and tied the straps.

She realised he was down to his boxer shorts. Green things with yellow bananas on them. They were tented from his excitement.

'You want one too?' she asked, trying to focus on something other than the depth of her emotions.

'Sure.'

Dorothy bent to reach into the kitchen drawer, a surprised sound escaping her when she felt a slap on her bottom.

'Couldn't resist,' Philip said cheekily, helping her stand.

'Here, what about this one?' Dorothy held out a navy blue apron. 'I think this would suit you. It matches your eyes.'

He took it from her and placed it over his head. 'What do you think?' he asked, turning around.

'Hold on, let me do the straps.' Dorothy pushed up close to his body and tied the straps at the back. 'I have to bend down again ... to get some sauce out of the freezer.' Her words were so breathy she wasn't sure he would understand her.

She bent. Philip moved. But this time, the touch was more caring. She almost forgot what she was doing, but eventually stood up, a package of homemade pasta sauce in her hands.

Eventually, Dorothy made supper and set it on the counter. Dorothy had never felt so alive, so vital and so glad to have a man around. She wasn't sure what was going to happen tonight, but she knew she liked what was happening now. And being a little more mature now, she felt she could be in charge. She was going to follow her own terms this time and not let guilt or some horny man dictate her actions, as she may have done in the past.

She set the large pasta bowl on the counter next to the smaller dishes they were going to eat out of. Philip picked up his fork and stuck it in the middle of the bowl.

'What are you doing?' Dorothy asked, startled. 'That's the serving dish!'

'Is it?' A cheeky smile pressed on Philip's face and he stuck the second fork in the same bowl. 'Try some.'

Dorothy laughed, but she took the second fork in her hand and wound some of the surrounding pasta.

'Delicious,' Philip said. He wasn't looking at the pasta. 'So, your mother taught you to cook?'

'Yes. Mum and I used to have competitions over who was going to cook supper. By the time I was eight or nine, I was roasting chickens and frying salmon.'

'Hmm...' Philip reached for the ramekin of olives on the side. He looked at her with his eyebrows arched as if asking if he could put them in the pasta. She gave a nod. 'Where did she learn?'

'She was a cook at a hotel in Cornwall,' Dorothy answered. 'She preferred the savoury dishes. I preferred the sweet.' She scooped some of the tomato sauce onto her fork. 'Hence the café.'

The olives fell into the pasta and Philip began mixing them in with his fork.

'Here,' Dorothy held out her own fork for him to take and continue mixing the food.

'We can do it together,' he said.

They did. It was a little odd, and the olives mostly stuck to one part of the bowl, but it was fun.

Philip watched Dorothy's fork, now holding a string of pasta. 'So, did you share the food with the other kids?' He leaned in, chewing on the same noodle until he earned a smile from Dorothy.

'I forgot the cheese,' Dorothy said, slightly breathless. 'Do you want...'

But Philip kissed her, stopping her from speaking. She lost her words as they shared the pasta noodle.

Minutes later, they separated, Philip saying, 'I can get the cheese.' He moved off the stool and went towards the fridge.

'So, what about you?' Dorothy asked. 'What were your favourite things to do when you were younger? Did you like to cook?'

Philip returned with a block of Parmesan cheese and a grater. 'Cook? No, I don't cook. Mum cooked because she had to. The kitchen wasn't really our place. Although Connie liked to; she'd make my lunches for me on the weekend. It wasn't elaborate or anything. You know, cheese on toast or a sandwich. But I liked it when she did.'

He poked an olive on his fork and held it out to Dorothy. She opened her lips and took it, savouring it in her mouth.

'Puzzles,' he said, watching the remaining pasta move in the bowl. 'I liked puzzles. Rubik's cubes, Monopoly ... all sorts. And crime books. And Operation. I was really good at that. I don't think it was the hand-eye coordination necessarily, but the idea of what went where and the shapes.'

Philip dug his fork into the pasta bowl and Dorothy emitted a laugh as he pulled his fork out at the same time she did and they held the same piece of spaghetti.

They soon finished eating, and after came an inevitable time of uncertainty. Having finished cleaning up, she stood in the kitchen, almost forgetting she was only in her lingerie and an apron.

'Dorothy, I like you.' He moved closer to her. 'A lot.'

She gave him a slight smile.

'But I don't know that staying tonight is a good idea,' he finished.

That wasn't what Dorothy wanted to hear. She stared at him, anger rising inside. 'So, you do all this,' she waved a hand towards him, 'and now you want to leave?'

'I'd like to be a gentleman and leave something for another time.'

'Gentleman?' Dorothy looked down to the floor, feeling a shiver of cold – or that's what she put it down to. 'No,' she said assertively. 'You take my clothes off, in my house, and now you want to leave?'

Philip stayed quiet, an intriguing expression on his face. He hadn't expected this reaction.

'You're not leaving!' She pulled him to her with the fabric of his navy apron. 'I'm not saying I want more and I'm not saying you must stay the night. But I am saying…' His finger trailed down her back and she shivered. 'You have to play at least one game of Jenga before we go through that mess of our clothes and figure out whose are whose.'

The smile grew back on Philip's face.

'I'll get the game. You fill the wine glasses,' Dorothy instructed.

Philip reached out to her and gave another kiss. 'I'm a champion of such measures.'

Dorothy moved into the living room, her hand pausing as she opened the game cupboard. She couldn't hear the wine being poured. In fact, it sounded like Philip had gone back to the front door. Perhaps she had been wrong and he needed to leave. She hoped not. To end the night that way would be a shame.

Fighting between fear that he would leave and the belief that he would stick around, she grabbed the game.

'I got something for you, Dorothy,' Philip said in a low voice as she moved back towards the kitchen.

She turned around.

'You weren't meant to, but I made a second card.' He held out a piece of light blue card. It was upside down, so she couldn't see the picture on it.

'That's very kind,' she stepped towards the table and placed the game down. Then she moved back to where Philip waited and took the card from him. Feelings of warmth brushed through her as she looked at the front of the card. It had feathers and doilies attached to it in the shape of an angel.

'I know you like the angel song ... "Hark the—"'

The words got swallowed up in the kiss Dorothy placed on his lips. She realised that the man in her arms really did like her. His act of not staying the night wasn't selfish, it was purely out of respect.

She set the card on the kitchen counter where they'd eaten their supper. 'You want more wine?' she asked quietly.

Philip gave a nod and moved to pour the drinks. He brought them over to the table. 'Ready for the champ to win?' he asked as he set the glasses down.

They played three games – he won two and Dorothy one won. After that, Philip insisted he had to leave, but he promised to see her tomorrow.

When they opened the front door, Philip predicted there would be snow by morning. He made her promise to go into work a little later, when he could walk her there. She said she'd see.

'I'll see you here tomorrow morning,' he promised with a deep, firm kiss.

Dorothy watched him cross the road. She didn't want to close the door.

Chapter Ten

Countdown Day 6

Seven days until Christmas

Dorothy shuffled around the kitchen. This morning, she had called May to tell her she'd be late to work. After getting ready and eating breakfast, she stood in the kitchen, preparing for Philip's arrival. Last night had been one of the strangest and most exhilarating nights of her life.

That's when she heard the thud.

She froze.

Then another one.

This time, she quirked an eyebrow and moved to where she thought the sound was coming from: the front door.

With a quizzical look, Dorothy opened the door.

It all happened at once. Something white flew towards her and she screamed as the snowball hit her front and left a damp patch.

She glared at where it had come from and found Philip standing a few feet away. Her visitor from last night wore a black wool coat, but no gloves or hat.

'Philip!'

Dorothy had some decisions to make.

She slammed the door shut, leaving him outside. She hurried into her coat, tied a scarf around her neck, wriggled her fingers into her gloves and pulled on her boots. Then she opened the door and closed it quickly behind her as she rushed outside.

Dorothy realised there wasn't much snow, but she planned to make the most of what little there was. She threw Philip a pair of black gloves in case he wanted to use them, then got to work, scooping some snow from the ground.

Philip, seeing her plan, put his hands up in surrender. 'Truce?'

Dorothy stood, her gloved hands forming a ball of snow, reflecting on when she'd opened her front door. *Now he's asking for a truce?*

'There's not much snow; we don't want to waste it,' Philip pointed out. 'Why don't we build a snowman?'

Dorothy considered it for several long seconds. 'Okay.'

The truce started with a good morning kiss and a wonderful hug. It moved into laughter as they rolled a small snowman's body, using the snow from the small patch of grass outside her own house, and the neighbour's.

Dorothy warmed Philip's hands by rubbing her own gloved hands on his, then using her extra pair of gloves to cover his fingers. All the while, their gazes met and, occasionally, more snow fell from the clouds.

'Catch the snow!' Dorothy cried, standing with her mouth open and tongue out to catch the snowflakes.

She felt Philip behind her. He gently turned her around before crashing his mouth on hers. Sparkles and tingles ran through her body.

And then came the phone call.

Philip stared at the screen, wide-eyed. He let the call ring out, not answering the phone, but the happy mood was broken.

Dorothy noticed his change in demeanour and, feeling slightly neglected and wanting to get him back in a playful spirit, encouraged, 'Let's take a selfie!'

A half-hearted cuddle and bend later (to get the tiny snowman in the picture), he stepped back. 'I have to go,' he said hesitantly.

Dorothy paused. She had thought he was going to walk her to work and was disappointed to leave his company so soon. Still, she swallowed and gave him the brightest smile she could muster as she said, 'Send the pictures to me.'

'I'll QR them on the photo board,' Philip responded.

Dorothy wasn't thinking about the Christmas Countdown; she just wanted the photos of them together. She stepped towards him and got lost in his eyes as he pulled her closer.

Still, Philip's face had shown horror when he saw that incoming call. What could that expression mean? Was it guilt? Was there another woman? Did he have someone else up in Manchester?

He gave her a gentle kiss, then his face rearranged as if he'd realised where he was. 'I'm sorry, I have to go,' he said abruptly.

Dorothy quickly stepped away from him, confused. Why hadn't he told her who had called or what had been bothering him? *I thought we were closer than that.*

He was still a good guy, though, and she was sure there was an explanation for the odd behaviour. She had to believe that.

The satisfaction of baking helped Dorothy enjoy the rest of the day. Kneading, whisking and cooking took her mind off the strange feeling she'd had about Philip that morning. By the end of the day, she had forgotten all about it.

Chapter Eleven

♥

Countdown Day 7

Six days until Christmas

The next day, she headed over to the bookshop, planning to speak to Oliver about the café and testing out a few business ideas. Though she now wondered if that was necessary. Perhaps she could ask Philip instead? He might shed a different light on them.

She'd had a couple of texts from him over the last day, reminding her that he'd not forgotten about her. She liked that.

As she entered the bookshop, it seemed empty; Oliver was nowhere to be seen. She moved to the back of the shop, where the rocking chair was, a familiar peaceful feeling visiting her. She sat in the chair and rocked slowly and comfortably.

What was really going on with her and Philip? Was it about respect or was it about another woman? Did it matter?

The funny thing about this chair, she determined, was the feelings she experienced when she sat in it and the questions that seemed to pop into her head. Like now, the thought occupying her mind was: *Do you like him?*

The question made sense, given the thoughts before it. So why wasn't it easy to answer? She liked being in his company and had enjoyed him staying for supper. He was fun, good-looking and had the kind of eyes that pulled her into oblivion when she looked into them.

What's not to like?

As she sat in the rocking chair, Dorothy heard voices at the front of the shop. She recognised them both: it was Oliver and Stephen.

'How's Philip's visit going?' Oliver asked.

Naturally, hearing the name *Philip* brought her out of her reverie. Dorothy perked up.

Part of her hoped they didn't see her sitting here or they might consider her eavesdropping. She didn't want that. She tried to get back to her thoughts, but she couldn't.

'Alright,' Stephen said. 'I haven't heard otherwise.' His voice was a lower volume than his father's. 'He's coming here to collect the sock box. We'll be collecting all the donations on Rosemary Road and the B&B and taking them to the hospital. We're meeting Mr Evans there.'

'It's been very popular,' Oliver commented.

'It has, hasn't it?' Stephen agreed. 'We might keep it going after Christmas.'

Moments later, Dorothy heard Philip's deep voice and her whole body buzzed in delight. Time slowed down as a jolt of the recent memories they'd made together flew through her: standing outside the café, playing board games at the community centre, exploring Eagle's Keep...

She could listen to that voice for hours.

Reinvigorated, she settled into the chair and rocked it a little more, staying there for a little longer than she'd intended.

Chapter Twelve

♥

D orothy pushed the restaurant door open and led the way into the wine bar. Philip had asked her on a date, but she had talked him out of going to the Italian restaurant in Sprawling Green, the main town closest to the village, suggesting they go there another time. The plan was for them to meet up with their friends later to see the Christmas lights, but the idea of going out in the cold made her want to wrap up warmly. So she said yes to the date but suggested saving the posh clothes for another time.

She had no doubts there would be another time.

'That one.' Philip pointed to a table at the back of the bar.

Dorothy obliged and walked over to it. It was a small table for two. The bar – a long room lined with wooden shelves filled with wine bottles – had a vintage feel to it. Dorothy looked around, absorbing the scene. She'd forgotten just how in awe she felt in this place.

Dorothy settled into the seat as Philip held the chair out for her. Of course he did. She wouldn't expect anything less from him.

'Cherry Corks...' Dorothy read as she opened the menu.

'Dorothy, I've got a question to ask you.' Philip leaned towards her, making her glance up from the menu. 'How am I going to rub my knee against yours if you're wearing such ... thick clothes? I suppose you've got extra layers underneath your trousers?'

Dorothy laughed, feeling his leg bump her knee under the table. She unwrapped herself from her padded winter coat and stuffed it behind her on the small metal chair.

'And those boots are rather ... clunky.' Philip gave her a mischievous look.

She unwound the scarf from her neck and removed her hat with a shake of her head. With the table feeling too small to accommodate them, she set the items on the floor, then reached for his hand. 'You can still touch me, Philip. I won't say no to that.'

He grinned back at her and leaned forwards. She met him with a small kiss.

They sat in silence for a moment before she said, 'I need help understanding something.'

He gave her a quizzical look, urging her to continue.

'Philip...' How was she going to say this? She didn't want to ruin the moment, but she needed answers. It fell from her lips: 'That phone call... Are you keeping a secret? Is there someone else?'

'What?' Philip moved his hand from her space, looking shocked. 'No!'

'Well then why did you leave me when your phone rang?' Dorothy glared at the little device on the table next to his cutlery setting.

'My family,' Philip answered slowly. 'I really don't—' He cut himself off. 'Let's not spoil this evening with talk of that. Please.'

But Dorothy wasn't satisfied. She didn't want to spoil their evening, but neither did she want to not mention it. Her thoughts tumbled around. She just wanted the truth, but she didn't feel he had given her that. Should she ask again?

But she was in a lovely place with a great man – someone who she found attractive in looks and personality – and she didn't want to throw that away by being pushy so early into their relationship.

She gave a long sigh, considering her next step. 'Tell me about your family,' she said finally.

This elicited a look almost as bad as the first question. She didn't stop or look away, though. Instead, she waited patiently, anticipating his reply.

'I don't get on with them,' Philip said, his voice low.

A server arrived at the table.

'We're not ready yet, thanks,' Dorothy said, earning a slightly surprised look from Philip.

'Not even for a drink?' the server persisted.

Philip looked at her, and she shook her head. 'It's a wine bar. There are so many to choose from. Can we have five minutes, please?' Even if Philip was ready, this topic was too important to ignore.

'Of course.' The server moved away.

Dorothy focused on Philip. 'You have a sister who's good at cooking, a mother who makes you uncomfortable and a father...?' When he said nothing, she continued, 'Something happened recently. What was that phone call about?'

Her voice was a touch stronger now. She wanted answers.

Philip gulped and looked away. 'I was hoping not to get into this today.'

'You and I have been getting along very well, but if I'm going to be with someone, I want tender moments. The vulnerabilities.'

'Right, well, lots of things happened a few weeks ago. My father ... he died,' Philip admitted. 'I didn't make it to the funeral and work dumped me.'

Dorothy blinked. She hadn't imagined that would be the cause of his secrecy! *Tread carefully here, Dorothy,* she told herself. She exhaled a breath as if on his behalf.

'I'm sorry.' He looked at her. 'For all of it. I'm sorry that happened.'

He heard the sincerity, and she squeezed his hand tighter.

'My father taught me ethics and loyalty. So, I assumed that meant to work hard all hours of the day. You allow nothing to get in the way. You don't become a pushover, but you work, work, work...' Philip said.

Dorothy nodded.

'I tried to get to the funeral, but I had an important meeting. It was in Manchester and I couldn't get away.' She watched his Adam's apple bob. 'My mum's not spoken to me since and my sister keeps calling me. She wants to talk. I don't. She's the entrepreneur. She goes out and starts businesses and I tell people how to run them. I have the qualifications; she has the true experience.' He made inverted commas with his fingers around the last word.

'Then, a few short weeks later, I screwed up at work, and they fired me. I had two clients with the same name and I got mixed up. I gave the wrong information to one of them and *boom!* You're out of work now, mate.'

Dorothy rose from her seat. She stepped over to Philip and wrapped her arms around him.

'That must have been so difficult,' she said. 'That's an awful lot to have happened. I'm so sorry,' she whispered in his ear.

They stayed that way for several long moments until she felt it was time to return to her seat. But she pulled the chair closer to his, rather than sitting opposite.

'If you don't want to talk about it anymore, it's okay,' she offered.

Philip heaved a deep sigh. 'Thank you, Dorothy.'

'Let's order,' Dorothy said. 'I know what food I want, but the wine... There are so many to choose from! What would you like?'

They ordered spicy meatballs, cheese batons and garlic bread – with no cheese, as she thought it tasted better that way.

Dorothy was so relieved that Philip had come clean with her but was heartbroken for him at the same time. The mix of emotions was so extreme that she wasn't sure she'd be able to eat anything.

'I commentate on the food when I eat out,' she told him. 'I can tell what herbs they use or how they cook it. I'm fussy that way. I went out with Abigail a few times when I first moved here and I kept doing it to the point where she got fed up with me. I'm better now.'

'You can critique their food tonight if you like,' Philip said, relaxing into the evening.

She let him choose the wine, a merlot. She liked his decisiveness around that. And it was a good choice; it tasted delicious.

They enjoyed an intimate and tasty meal, then asked for the bill.

'I can pay my share,' Dorothy offered, reaching for her bag – another chunky item, easy to wrap over her shoulder and keep close when they were walking.

'You'll do no such thing!' Philip said, reaching for his wallet.

'Thank you,' Dorothy said.

See, even if we're not in a posh restaurant he can still be romantic, she thought to herself, happy with how the evening had gone so far. The taste of his honesty was enough for now. She knew those experiences must have been difficult, especially all at once. She found herself wanting to make him feel better for the sadness he was entrenched in.

Chapter Thirteen

♥

Countdown Day 8

Five days until Christmas

A wave of happiness visited Dorothy as she and Philip walked hand-in-hand by the riverside on the way to meet their friends. The evening was chilly, and she was glad to be wearing all her layers, despite Philip's earlier teasing.

The road took the shape of an upside-down T leading up a hill to the library and council buildings in Sprawling Green.

'There they are!' Abigail waved to the couple as they approached, then rushed over to them. 'I was hoping... Oh, you look so...' she tripped over her words as she looked at Dorothy's and Philip's linked arms, then eventually finished with, 'I hope you had a good time.'

Dorothy was sure her cheeks had heated, despite the temperature. 'We had a lovely time, thank you. Who else is here?'

The same gang who had been in her café greeted her, with the addition of another couple whose names Dorothy forgot as soon as they were spoken, and several of Abigail's children. She smiled at them all.

Oliver's eyes twinkled as he acknowledged Dorothy. She felt he looked particularly distinguished tonight as he leaned on his black and red walking cane.

'Doesn't it look beautiful?' Abigail asked, turning her back to the river and pointing up the hill.

Dorothy followed her gaze. The main street in Sprawling Green was lit up with yellow sparkly lights. Green and silver banners adorned with the town's logo were draping from the lamp posts, which were emanating an inviting glow.

'So, it's just this street in the Countdown?' Cameron asked at an unusually lowered volume. 'How did that go down in the planning?'

'There was some fuss,' Oliver answered. 'We wanted to mostly showcase Lavender Village, but this view is so beautiful, we couldn't resist.' He waved a hand towards the river.

Dorothy absorbed the picture, a reflection of the golden orb of the moon and twinkly lights from the streetlights. She suspected it was Oliver who couldn't resist, and the other committee members could have lived without including the town. But they had conceded for the shops on Churchill Street to be included in the countdown. If they hadn't, she probably wouldn't be standing here now.

'Let's cross the road, then,' Abigail said excitedly. 'There's a bit more space over there, and the view is even better!'

They pushed the traffic light button and crossed the street to the pedestrian-only section of Churchill Street.

'So, why is it called Sprawling Green?' Philip asked as they crossed. 'That's an odd name for a town.'

Oliver chuckled, and Stephen answered, 'It's actually named that because of the fields around the town. Did you notice there were no other towns or villages on the way here?'

Philip contemplated the question. He'd driven and Dorothy had given him directions. 'I was driving,' he answered honestly.

'It's like a wheel. There are four roads like spokes into the main artery – or the town, in this case. The surrounding villages are separate to Sprawling Green. There's a green belt and farm land around it, so if more people come or anyone wants to build, they can't. They must use the buildings they already have here.'

'So they'll never build on it? That's good,' Philip said, pulling out his mobile phone. He turned to Dorothy. 'Would you like to take some photos with my phone?'

Dorothy's face brightened. 'That would be brilliant. Thank you.' She removed one of her gloves and took the mobile. 'Look!' She pointed to the bottom of the hill and the water, where there was a mass of glowing lights. 'It's like a scene from a fairy tale or a romantic film.'

Philip turned around. The incredible wonder of Sprawling Green's river with the moon and streetlight banners met his eyes. He could understand why Oliver wanted to include this spot in the Christmas festivities. He wrapped an arm around Dorothy just as she announced, 'Selfie!' and held his phone in front of them.

Dorothy moved away from Philip, not intentionally, but because she was so absorbed in snapping photos.

Abigail moved over to her. 'It's all so...'

'Ooey-gooey,' Dorothy finished triumphantly, wrapping an arm around her friend. 'Makes you feel ooey-gooey inside.'

'I know,' Abigail agreed. 'I love Christmas.'

'Oh!' Dorothy looked down at the vibrating phone in her hand. 'It's a call. No, a message.' For a tiny flicker of a second, Dorothy wondered if it was from a woman up in Manchester.

She looked around for Philip. He was talking to Oliver. Should she tell him? That would be the decent thing. But she was saved from the worry. Philip looked to her and Abigail, then moved over to them.

'You've got a text message,' Abigail explained.

He took the phone, pressed a button and glanced at the screen. 'It's from Liz Montgomery. The Medieval Society.' He smiled. 'I asked about joining the jousting group for next summer.'

'Oh, that's great,' Dorothy congratulated Philip, pleasantly surprised that he was making plans to visit Lavender Village over the summer. And perhaps he'd come to visit over the upcoming months, too. A warm feeling stirred inside her.

'Brilliant!' Abigail added.

'Lean in,' Philip said, holding the phone in front of their faces, wanting to take a photo.

Dorothy and Abigail obliged, then Abigail excused herself, moving over to her family.

The larger than usual crowd – as a result of Abigail's family joining them – meant it was harder for them to stay together, and as they walked along the high street, several people split off to go into various shops. Dorothy felt it was three groups rather than just her and her friends, but that determined more fun and excitement for the occasion.

'You want more pictures?' Philip asked Dorothy in a moment when they found themselves alone, offering his phone out to her.

'Thanks.' Dorothy held out her hand, but he kept hold of the phone for an extra second, causing her to glance up at him.

'Did I tell you, you look beautiful tonight?' Philip asked.

A touch of heat reddened her cheeks. 'Thank you.'

He released the phone into her hand and together they moved up the road, which was decorated with festive decorations and criss-cross lights. Dorothy clicked away happily, getting as many photographs of the group as she could. She also made sure to capture the prettily decorated shops.

As she snapped away, she noticed Isabel exiting a dress shop, clutching a garment bag in her hands. Her smiley face was filled with excitement.

Oliver and Stephen reached Dorothy and Philip, and Oliver nodded towards Hugo's, a large bookshop to their left. 'I'm just going in here,' he said.

'What?' Cameron spluttered. 'The competition?'

'Seems so!' Oliver chortled, moving towards the door. 'If you need Christmas Countdown stamps...'

The group chuckled.

'Not a bad idea,' Angus said.

Cameron glared at his brother. 'Traitor!'

'You stay out here in the cold.' Angus prepared to pass his brother, holding a hand out to Sophie, who took it. 'But we're going in.'

Dorothy felt a rush of warm air as she followed the couple. Once inside, she shook her curls out of her hat, relishing in the warmth of the shop.

She heard the door open behind her and was surprised when Philip followed her in, taking her hand and saying, 'Come with me!'

'Oh!' Dorothy replied, surprised. 'Alright.'

'I was going to do it as a surprise and meet you back downstairs, but this will have to do.'

Dorothy smiled, slightly confused. 'Which way?'

He led her towards the back of the shop and glanced towards the stairs. Then, at the last moment, he whisked her towards the lift. 'This way!' he said when the doors opened, and together they entered the lift.

As the doors closed, Philip turned to Dorothy. 'Quiet at last,' he whispered, looking into her eyes. He leaned forwards and kissed her. A warm, gallant kiss which she happily reciprocated.

The lift stopped and they heard voices on the other side of the doors. Dorothy separated from him just in time as the doors parted to reveal a family with two small children and a pushchair.

'Come on,' Philip said, finding her hand as they moved past the family. 'This way.'

Moments later, they stood at what Dorothy would have described as the mature section. She felt herself blush.

'Ah.' Philip pulled a book from a shelf. It had a red and white cover.

Dorothy quickly scanned the title: *Love, Romance and 100 Ways to Show It.* She smiled at him. 'You think we need this now?'

Philip nodded. 'It gives tips and cues on romance.' He opened the book and held it out to her. 'Look, it talks about kitchens too.'

'Okay...' Dorothy said, slowly. 'And you're getting this for us?'

'Mm hmm.' Philip nodded, giving her a quick kiss on her nose, still cold from the winter air. 'Us.'

'Alright. That's very kind,' Dorothy replied.

Philip wrapped an arm around her and squeezed affectionately.

They took the stairs down, purchased the book and rejoined their friends. Dorothy didn't share the purchase with the group. Instead, she tucked it safely into her bag, feeling it was something she wanted to keep between the two of them.

'Would you like my phone?' Philip asked Dorothy as they stepped outside.

'Not yet,' Dorothy said. 'I have a question. What's your favourite Christmas memory?'

Philip frowned. 'That's a hard one.' They walked a few paces. 'What's yours?'

'The December before my parents died, twelve years ago. We all went on holiday together. It wasn't very often we did that, with me being an adult and our work schedules. Anyway, we stayed in a cottage not far from here, in the Cotswolds. It had a pink door.' Her face took on a dreamy smile. 'It was fun, being just us. They died a few months later.' She looked at Philip. 'That's my favourite memory.'

Philip stopped walking and turned to Dorothy. 'Hey,' he said softly.

She smiled back, and he bent down and gave her a tender kiss.

Moments later, Cameron wolf whistled and shouted, 'Can't you wait 'til you get back?'

Dorothy and Philip parted to see Isabel pulling Cameron's head towards hers and giving him a kiss.

'I'm sorry about your parents,' Philip said, ignoring the interruption.

Dorothy nodded in thanks for his sweet gesture.

'More photos?' Philip asked, and Dorothy felt his hand next to her body as he took his phone out of his pocket.

She took her gloves off and put them into her bag, then accepted the mobile. She turned back to see the silver banners on the street lights and twinkles of lights criss-crossing over the road ahead of them. 'It's so beautiful,' she breathed.

'Yeah, and the river,' Philip agreed, pointing to the river and the bridge crossing it, which was similarly decorated.

They stood for several moments, enjoying the soft, luminescent glow. And as if to perfect the night, snowflakes began to dance down, catching the light as they fell, creating a shimmering curtain of silver that enveloped the world in a gentle embrace.

Dorothy took more photos of Philip and her friends, delighting in the season's atmosphere and feeling endlessly grateful for the Christmas Countdown. A thought occurred to her then: If she hadn't participated in the activities, she'd never have got so close to Philip.

Maybe, just maybe, this thing between us could work, she thought as she snapped another picture of him and her friends.

Chapter Fourteen

♥

Countdown Day 9

Four days until Christmas

I t was a strange phenomenon, being part of the Countdown activities. Dorothy found herself increasingly keen to see her friends and take part in the activities.

Tonight was no different. She sat in the community centre next to Philip – who had met her with a very long, deep kiss – waiting for a murder mystery event to begin. The local theatre group had invited a company who were promoting their services, and a special Christmas mystery was about to begin.

There were two conditions: you had to dress in an item of Christmas-themed clothing, and you had to have a pre-paid ticket. They had reduced the price significantly as the actors were volunteering their time for the occasion, but the cost of getting the company to the show had to be covered. It proved to be a very popular idea, as the tickets had sold out in fifteen minutes.

She sat down next to a large, friendly woman whose name she knew but couldn't draw until the very last moment.

'Hello, Elsie,' Dorothy said, a flicker of relief passing through her upon recalling.

'Dorothy! How are you?'

'Very well, thank you.'

'I'm wearing my Christmas earrings.' Elsie pointed to the snowman earrings swinging from her ears.

'I can't see; they're swinging too fast!' Dorothy said with a chuckle.

Elsie stilled one with her fingers and Dorothy laughed at the little snowman dangling there.

'It's great!' Dorothy said. 'I went with a scarf and Christmas colours.' She pointed to the blue scarf with silver and white snowflakes printed on it. Her hand moved down to her glitzy silver top, which met her jeans. She'd realised after going through her wardrobe that she didn't have a Christmas jumper. She had made a note to change that next year.

'I see you're with someone.' Elsie looked at the man on Dorothy's other side.

'Oh, this is Philip. He's ... visiting for Christmas. He's a friend of Stephen's.'

At that, Philip switched off his phone and slid it into his pocket. 'Philip Ray,' he added, greeting Elsie.

'Elsie Ryder.'

'Good to meet you.'

'Elsie lives on Mulberry Lane, just at the other end. In the corner house.'

'The one with the flowers and Christmas decorations outside?' Philip asked.

'Yes! I love my flowers.'

A wash of surprise fell over Dorothy. She rarely went that far down the road; there was no need, and she certainly hadn't taken Philip past Elsie's house. He must have taken a walk while getting to know the neighbourhood. She hadn't expected that, but she was glad he was attempting to get to know Lavender Village.

'Have you been to one of these before?'

'Never,' Dorothy answered at the same time as Philip replied, 'Yes.'

'Me neither,' Elsie said, just as a voice called from behind them. They all turned to see Abigail waving from two rows back.

'Hello!' Abigail was wearing a bright green jumper with a Christmas pattern on it. 'We only got five tickets,' Abigail whisper-shouted, pointing to her family. Practically everyone in the seats between watched Abigail for her explanation. 'We had a bit of a fight about who would come, and we won.' Abigail pointed to herself, her granddaughter, and a couple of other family members sitting in the row, then gave a thumbs up.

'Oh, goodness!' Dorothy said, sensing Philip's leg pushing against hers. She liked it. A buzzing sensation in her body made her want to reciprocate wildly.

'See you later,' Abigail said over the hum of the voices as people went back to their conversations. Dorothy was about to turn around when Abigail mouthed the words, *Don't leave without seeing me, please.*

Dorothy squinted, missing what her friend had said.

But Elsie came to the rescue. 'She wants to see us afterwards,' she supplied.

'Oh, okay.' Dorothy nodded vehemently.

A voice boomed through the microphone. It wasn't Mr Cleese's; it was a fresh, fun, professional voice who introduced himself and the theatre group.

The evening began.

-x-

'That was a load of fun!' Elsie said as they moved with the crowd towards the doors.

'It was,' Dorothy agreed. 'I didn't have a clue who stole Father Christmas's bells. I loved that it was appropriate for children, too. They seemed to really enjoy it. And well done, Philip. You barely had three clues and you got the answer!'

'Hello!' Abigail smiled, approaching the trio as they stood outside in the chilly night air. 'Do you want to come for supper? We've got loads of food.'

'Can't say no to that smile,' Elsie said.

As they moved down the road with Abigail's family, Dorothy felt Philip touch her back. He had seemed more affectionate tonight than he had at the meal. But then, the topic of conversation had been heavy that night.

They soon reached Abigail's house and all filtered inside. Dorothy watched the crowd with a smile. A hum of conversation rang around the walls as they all tucked into a chilli that Abigail had made. It was delicious, all absorbed with non-cheesy garlic bread which complemented the dish perfectly.

She smiled as she watched Philip talking to one of Abigail's sons. She poured herself another glass of wine and pondered asking Philip to stay with her tonight.

Tingles ran through her body at the thought. What was it with this man?

She remembered sitting on the chair in her hallway and wondered if they would make it upstairs this time. Would he say no again, or was the time right?

Maybe they could run around the house half naked again...

'Dorothy,' Oliver said, startling her.

Dorothy turned to him. 'Oliver, how are you?'

'I'm well, thank you,' Oliver said. Then he leaned over and said in a low voice, 'Love is the condition in which the happiness of another person is essential to your own.'

'Sorry?' Dorothy blinked.

'A quote from Robert A. Heinlein.' Oliver pointedly followed where Dorothy's gaze had been: on Philip.

'Oh,' Dorothy felt her face heat and looked down at the floor. 'I'm not sure about that.'

'I used to say it to Claire, my late wife.'

'Oh, right.' Dorothy looked back at him with a smile.

'Ah, excuse me, I'd like to chat with Serena.' He leaned in again and added, 'Somehow, when I talk to her, she doesn't push me off and tell me it's time to go home. For a while, anyway.'

Dorothy smiled but felt a tinge of sadness. She put a gentle hand on his arm and he looked at her with large, round eyes. 'Have a lovely Christmas, Oliver.'

'Thank you. You too, dear.'

With that, he moved towards Serena, Abigail's daughter. Dorothy took another swig of wine and headed towards Philip.

'How much of a gentleman are you feeling tonight?' she asked Philip, catching him as he stepped away from his conversation.

He faltered, a grin spreading on his face.

'What I'm really asking is, do you want to stay the night with me?' She paused. 'Even if we just run upstairs in cooking aprons and our—'

Philip's lips met hers, and she had her answer.

'...underwear,' she said breathily, finishing her sentence. 'We could just lie on the bed together. We don't—'

'You've got your answer,' Philip replied. It sounded more like a grunt. 'I was going to have a whiskey but that can wait for another time. Let's go,' he said, whispering in her ear as he slung an arm around her.

Chapter Fifteen

♥

Countdown Day 10

Three days until Christmas

Dorothy didn't want to accept the stabs of inadequacy as a result of Philip hurrying out that morning with barely any breakfast in his stomach.

Luckily, she didn't have too much time to think about it, as the café was particularly busy today. They finished another ink pad for the stamps and sold more of Abigail's snow globes.

Tonight, the café was holding Family Film Night as part of the Christmas Countdown. They'd be open a little later than usual, with the film starting at half past five this evening. It was only a short animated movie, so it would finish at six o'clock, and after clean-up she and the staff would hopefully be done for the day by half-past.

May and Brian had moved the tables in the dining area to allow for the viewing of the film on the stand-up projector screen which she had borrowed from a friend. Her iPad and Netflix were organised and ready to go, thanks to Brian. All she had to do was click play.

'Alright, the food is ready. It's self-serve biscuits, cake slices and popcorn,' Dorothy said to her employees. She looked at the popcorn wagon in the corner, which issued a delicious smell in the café. 'Everything is in packages so there shouldn't be much waste and clean-up will be quicker. We've got paper plates, plastic cups, China mugs and glasses. The glasses are for the juice if they don't want to drink out of a bottle. They can take the mugs away, but don't let them take the glasses. Okay?'

She paused to wait for questions, but no one spoke, so she continued, 'May, you're on hot drinks. Brian, you're doing entry and Christmas Countdown stamps. It's two pounds per person, no matter what they eat or how many they have.'

Her employee nodded. Brian looked unusually happy. Dorothy didn't spend time pondering why. She had enough on her mind.

'Brian, if I have any technical issues, I'll be asking you for help.' Brian's smile widened. 'The film is half an hour long. I've got a backup if something goes wrong.' Dorothy moved a hand in the air as if rubbing away thoughts of anything going wrong. She forced a smile, despite the tummy flutters. 'Let's not discuss that. We won't need it, right?'

-x-

Later, as she waited for people to enter for the film showing, Dorothy wondered what had made Philip leave so quickly this morning. It was hardly a great confidence booster.

'Dorothy?' Abigail asked.

'Sorry?' She got the impression her friend had tried to get her attention more than once.

'Snow globes: do you need more?'

The snow globes were selling well, and Stephen had brought some more since their discussion in the community centre.

The spell over Dorothy slid away. 'Yes, please. Either one.'

Abigail dug into her bag and pulled out three more of her snow globes. As she handed them over, she asked, 'Dorothy? Are you alright?'

Dorothy hesitated, biting her lower lip. 'Philip stayed over last night.'

Abigail gave a nod, clearly not surprised by this news. 'Okay...'

'He left. In a hurry.'

Abigail frowned but waited for her friend to continue.

'I don't like that,' Dorothy said simply. The degree of her dislike went deeper than she cared to admit. But before she could hear Abigail's reaction, a group of people entered the café.

Dorothy moved her attention to the newcomers. 'Hello. Are you here for the film?'

They nodded.

'Well, you're in the right place. Tonight is going to work slightly differently. It's self-serve, with food on the tables, and we have hot drinks available on that side.' She pointed to where a smiling May waited. 'Find a seat, help yourselves and enjoy the film.'

'What's the film?' one of them asked.

'Oh, *Shaun the Sheep*, the Christmas one.' Dorothy had had a hard time finding it, but was glad she had, as she knew it would be a crowd-pleaser.

Hearing the café's door swing open, Dorothy glanced over, surprised to see Philip enter. She let him wait for a moment, continuing to talk to the group and point them to their seats.

Once they were settled, she walked over to Philip. 'Hi,' she said simply.

'Hi.' He seemed to be back in his stoic persona. 'How are you?'

Dorothy's eyebrows knitted. 'I'm okay. How's your day been?'

'Yeah, I ... went for a walk.' Slowly, he leaned down and gave her a brief kiss on the cheek. It all felt rather silly. Stiff, awkward and uncomfortable. Irritation and regret ran through Dorothy. She shouldn't have asked him to stay last night.

What a ridiculous idea that was, she thought. *Won't happen in a hurry again. He's going home soon, anyway.*

'Excuse me,' Dorothy said, moving away from him to a new group that had entered the café. 'Find a seat,' she called over her shoulder.

A few minutes later, the film started. The café was full, but the noise quieted as people focused on the film, laughing along to the comedic story. Despite her earlier disappointment over the situation with Philip, Dorothy felt glad that she'd hosted tonight.

Close to the end of the film, a commotion erupted as someone's drink fell on the floor. Dorothy moved over the mess, passing Philip on her way. She noted he had his phone pressed to his ear, mumbling into it.

Dorothy set about cleaning the floor where the drink had spilled. When she had finished, she stood up and looked around the café. There was no sign of Philip, and irritation poked at her again.

She was headed towards the kitchen when Abigail stopped her. 'Philip had to go. He asked me to tell you,' she informed her.

Dorothy nodded at her friend but didn't say a word. Instead, she moved into the kitchen to put the cleaning things away. No tears came, only anger.

The kitchen door opened and Abigail asked, 'Dorothy, are you okay?'

'What are you doing here?' she asked her friend. She softened her tone, not wanting to take her anger out on the messenger. 'You're not supposed to be back here, and you're missing the film.'

Abigail ignored the rules and put a gentle hand on her friend's back. 'He's having family troubles,' she said softly.

'Family troubles?' Dorothy spat. 'If that's the case, why can't he tell me instead of walking out and saying goodbye through you!'

Abigail gave her a sympathetic look.

'I thought he wasn't in touch with them,' Dorothy said. Still no tears, just a sunken feeling of disappointment. 'See? I was right. Men just... He's not worth it. He only thinks of himself. It was a short, quick thing. That's it.'

Abigail's arm wrapped around Dorothy 'Hey, that's not true.'

'I always thought I was too busy to date, but it's not that. I just didn't want the humiliation of this. I'm going to tidy up, and when the film is finished I'll lock up and head home.'

Abigail opened her arms to hug her friend, but Dorothy shook her head and turned, beginning to tidy up instead.

Abigail turned to leave, but paused, saying, 'Now's the time he needs you most, Dorothy.'

How can he, when he's not even talking to me? Dorothy wondered bitterly.

Chapter Sixteen

♥

Countdown Day 11

Two days until Christmas

D orothy hid in the kitchen of the café, but with good reason, she justified. The place was busy. She suspected the bookshop being so close to them had something to do with it.

Today, the bookshop was hosting the Countdown activity. Throughout the day they were offering various Christmas book readings based on the different ages of the listeners. Younger ones first – naptime accounted for – and the main event Christmas reading later that day.

She was still feeling anguish over the state of her relationship with Philip, and talking about things didn't help. She didn't know who to talk to, anyway. Abigail, she supposed. But her friend's cosy home was always filled with her family and had little privacy. And the café was like home to her, but too public.

No, she would stay here in the kitchen. Three deliveries had arrived at the cafe today and Dorothy was feeling the need to bake. And whip up a storm, she did. Brian was overwhelmed with the number of biscuits and yule logs she had made, and May commented that they had never seen so many cakes on the counter.

'We're running out of space, Dorothy,' she said at one point.

'Take one home!' Dorothy retorted.

May blinked and set two of the yule logs aside, before looking at Brian and asking, 'You want one?'

'I can't take all of it,' Brian said sheepishly. 'Me mam'll say I nicked it.'

May smiled. 'Here.' She began cutting the yule logs into pieces. 'We'll give them away as free samples around the tables.'

Brian swallowed, clearly thinking, *Like I don't have enough to do.*

'We don't need signs,' May said as she watched Brian's gaze travel to the pens and stickers on the shelf. 'Yule logs. That's all they need to know. And take a slice or two for yourself and your mum.' May reached for a large aluminium to-go tray and stuck two chunks of yule log in the container. Then she grabbed a handful of biscuits and set them around the thick pieces. 'There, tell your mum it's a Christmas present from Dorothy.'

When Brian tried to protest, she said, 'There's plenty here. We can't eat all of it, and neither can the customers.'

Brian smiled and thanked May. All the while, Dorothy kept baking.

-x-

'Dorothy, we're leaving now!' May called from the doorway to the kitchen.

'What's that?' Dorothy moved from the oven to the front of the shop. Seeing her employees in their coats she asked, 'Is it six o'clock already?'

'Yes,' May said simply.

'Oh, I lost track of time today! Have a good evening.' A timer rang and Dorothy stepped back to the oven. 'We're leaving early tomorrow, alright?'

That earned smiles and quick exits, which Dorothy barely took note of. She returned to the German strudel cakes with a happy sigh. Compared to earlier, she was feeling much lighter than when she'd arrived. Baking always helped.

Now to consider attending the last Christmas story reading. She glanced at the clock. Plenty of time to clean up and get there. The question was, did she want to go?

If you had asked at nine o'clock this morning, she'd have said no. But now, many hours and zillions of bakes later...

Well, maybe she did.

She danced around the kitchen, scooping up the dirty bowls she'd created. A whole new mood visited her. She was Dorothy Wise. She was a successful business owner and perfectly competent baker, thank you very much. She was not going to allow anyone to upset her. And certainly not some guy who had stayed the night and ignored her afterwards. No.

'Damn!' she cursed as the spray arm slipped from her fingers and splashed the wall, dousing her with water. Her mood fell a little, but she continued washing the pots and bowls.

Did she still want to go to the bookshop?

She dried her hands, nodded to her kitchen to thank it for all its service and moved down the passageway. Of course, she'd go – if only to see the chair.

-x-

The bookshop was packed, yet Dorothy felt that familiar feeling of comfort and being in the right place. She gravitated to the rocking chair, and her entry through the crowd was nothing short of miraculous. People parted to let her through, a mother with a pushchair even moving to make room for her.

She reached the chair, which was occupied by two small boys bickering over who would sit in it. One suddenly burst into tears, which earned him a glare from a woman – presumably their mother – who promptly pulled both boys away from the chair.

It left the chair vacant.

As Dorothy sat in the rocking chair, feelings of shock and gratitude visited her. She closed her eyes and released a sigh. She wasn't sure which story was going to be read today, but she looked forward to hearing Oliver Livingstone's voice, nonetheless.

But it wasn't his voice who greeted the crowd. It was Stephen's.

Stephen sat on the bay window bench and spoke to the group: 'Ladies and gentlemen, welcome and thank you for coming. It has been a crazy ten days or so, but lots of Christmas spirit has been shared...'

Stephen went on, but Dorothy zoned out, consumed by an odd feeling. Curiosity? No. Not quite.

She turned her head and there stood Philip. She pursed her lips and looked to the front again.

'Tonight, I'm going to read *A Christmas Carol* by a famous British author, Charles Dickens. This story runs with themes of forgiveness, kindness and empathy. After all, it is Christmas time.'

And he began to read.

Dorothy tried to concentrate on the words, but thoughts exploded in her head. Unkind thoughts which she wasn't sure she was meant to have while sitting in the chair, especially so close to Christmas.

She gripped her hands together, pushing the tension out of her. But then she sensed someone close by. Blinking her eyes open, she saw Philip had moved closer to her.

Was that his touch she felt on her shoulder? What was he trying to do? Flashes of anger scorched through her, but they were quickly replaced with the memory of their connection.

Of laughing and drinking wine in her home.

Of Philip standing in the café, supporting her after dealing with that angry man.

Of their night together, before everything had gone wrong.

Stephen told the group about the second ghost appearing in front of Scrooge. Was she a Scrooge?

Surely not! She was just feeling awkward at the sudden change in her relationship with Philip.

What will I do if he tries to speak to me tonight? she wondered. *Be polite, Dorothy. Just be polite,* she coached herself.

'Thank you all very much for coming,' Stephen's voice echoed through the bookshop as the story came to an end. 'We wish you all a happy Christmas!'

Chatter began as people awoke from the cosiness of a finished story. The crowd began to stir and move out of the bookshop.

'Dorothy,' a voice behind her spoke. It was low, husky. She almost didn't hear it.

Taking a deep breath, she turned towards Philip. 'Hi.'

'I've been trying to contact you today.'

'Oh, I've not checked my messages,' she said. It was true. She wasn't sure she'd even turned on her phone.

'Can we talk now?' Philip asked, brow furrowed.

Inside, Dorothy cringed. Emotions jostled like a tug-of-war rope. *Yes* meant hearing some truths. *No* meant not giving them a chance.

'Alright,' she said eventually, staying seated while the people around them filtered out.

'The other night…' Philip began, once they were alone.

Dorothy's insides sank. This was where he was going to brush her off, she was certain.

'… was great,' Philip finished. 'I'm so glad we spent it together.'

A small, surprised smile sat on her face. She reached for his hand. The words were lost in her, but with the motion she conveyed the same sentiment.

'My family has been contacting me.' He sounded strained. Dorothy waited. 'My sister—'

Suddenly, Isabel appeared around the end of the bookshelves. 'Hey, guys! I wasn't sure if anyone was still here. We're just locking up.' She pointed in the direction of the doors.

'Oh, of course.' Dorothy stood, and in doing so, she released Philip's hand.

They moved to the front of the bookstore, bidding Isabel goodbye. Once they were outside, Dorothy tried to continue the conversation: 'Your sister?'

'Yeah…' That stoic expression had returned.

Dorothy wasn't sure she wanted to risk being hurt again, but Christmas was about forgiveness. 'You want to come to mine?' she managed.

'I can't,' Philip said. 'I've got to be at the station.'

'The station?' Dorothy repeated.

Philip nodded.

'Why?'

But it was too late. The cold air registered for the first time since stepping outside as Philip moved towards the black car he had arrived in. Shooting her a regretful look as he opened the car door, he said, 'I have to go. I'm sorry.'

Chapter Seventeen

♥

Countdown Day 12

Christmas Eve

T he young soloist stepped forward and began his song, "Away in a Manger."

Dorothy smiled, and something inside her melted. This night – when the local choir sang as they walked through the village – was always so beautiful. The wonderful thing about this evening was that you got to hear so many voices. The choir started it off, but everyone could join in.

They did it every year, usually starting on the other side of the bridge, but since Eagle's Keep was on the Christmas Countdown list, they had started there instead. A handful of people were already present – mostly the choir's family or people who had accompanied them at the start.

The song finished and Jayden Perry put a hand through his floppy hair to move it from his eyes as he addressed the crowd. 'Good evening, ladies and gentlemen. Thank you for coming out on this chilly night! We are the Lavender Village Choir, an award-winning non-denominational group.'

He paused while the gathered crowd applauded. Dorothy thought his voice sounded slightly sing-song, even when he wasn't singing.

'Our members are wearing blue cloaks.' He lifted the fabric of his bright blue cloak. 'And we'll be walking from here to the community centre. We have a set programme and song sheets if you would like one, but if you'd like a choice of song, let us know when we get there and we'll accommodate.'

Jayden looked at a group of the singers on the left and held his arm up. 'Okay, let's continue. And feel free to join in,' he said, giving a nod to the crowd.

'*Ding Dong Merrily...*' the women's voices began, and everybody moved towards the bridge.

A sense of peace settled over Dorothy as she followed them over the bridge. She loved hearing the sounds of a well-sung song and she'd always fancied herself as a bit of a singer, so she joined in.

An hour to sing and enjoy Christmas Eve. This would be fantastic.

They progressed over the bridge to meet the people lining Rosemary Road. People stood outside the shops, most of which were closed by now. There was only one open: the fish and chip shop.

Dorothy smiled and inhaled the smell of fried food. She considered joining the queue to get some chips, but decided it was a waste to miss the choir.

The song finished and Jayden led his choir to the next pit-stop. 'Welcome, ladies and gentlemen...' He began his spiel again, but his charisma made it sound different each time, keeping the crowd engaged.

Dorothy looked at the people crowding the choir: Abigail, Isabel, Cameron, Sophie, Angus, and even Oliver – the old man stooping with his cane. There were more people surrounding Abigail, including a smaller child. Her family, of course. Dorothy had forgotten they had all come to visit.

Strangely, despite her reluctance to look for him, Dorothy felt a sense of disappointment that she couldn't see Philip. But, of course, he'd gone home. Left the village to continue his life in Manchester.

Ridiculous! she told herself. Why was she thinking about him?

Stephen approached from her right, crossing through the crowd, carrying two large plastic bags of food.

'Yes!' a child shouted. 'Food!'

'Shh!' someone whispered to the child. It seemed a lull between songs had coincided with the child's outburst.

Moments later, the rustle of bags and paper issued and Jayden looked around, as if waiting for the next best time to begin.

'Hello.' Dorothy waved to her friends, glad to see them all. Greetings met her, and she took the initiative to grab some of the paper carol sheets that were being passed around, along with the parcels of food.

Jayden raised his arms again, and the choir restarted.

Two things happened at once: Dorothy smelled fish and chips very close to her, and someone said, 'Hello.'

She recognised that voice.

'Philip!' she said, surprised. 'What's going on?'

'Thought you'd like some?' He held out the package to her.

Emotions twisted inside Dorothy. The smell was so strong; how could she resist? But she really needed to discuss some things first before they started to pretend everything was fine between them.

The delicious smell wafted under her nose as he stuck his hand into the package and pulled out a chip. She had to look away, her mouth watering.

'We need to talk, Philip,' Dorothy said, forcing the words out through the confusion of her thoughts.

'Mmm perfectly vinegary,' he said, looking at her. 'I like vinegar on chips. I know you do, too.' She'd told him that the other night.

More memories pushed forwards. They'd run around the house again. They'd touched. They'd stayed up talking. They'd spent the night together. They'd done more than the first night, but still he'd been 'a gentleman', in his words.

'Perhaps we should have done more!' Dorothy blurted, causing several people to turn towards them.

'What?' Philip said through his mouthful.

'Perhaps I should have gone the whole hog and maybe then...' Dorothy lowered her voice, 'you wouldn't have ignored me these last few days.'

'I'm glad you didn't,' Philip said. 'I would have ignored you anyway.'

'What?' She was taken aback. 'Why?'

'Because I was trying to sort out my family,' Philip said. 'I heard from my sister and mother.'

While having this stunted conversation, they'd been slowly following the crowd around the corner. Jayden stopped a second time to collect more people, and Dorothy felt it best to stay quiet as he spoke to the new joiners.

Philip took two chips from the package and held them out to her. 'Please,' he said, his voice low.

She swallowed deeply, then accepted them. She closed her eyes as she chewed them. For something so simple, they really were delicious.

'I've missed you, Dorothy,' Philip whispered.

'Why didn't you call me?' Dorothy replied. 'And why did you rush out on me yesterday? I thought you were leaving without saying good-bye.'

'No!' Philip said just as "Jingle Bells" began and a lady next to them started ringing a set of bells and singing loudly. 'I... Look, this isn't a good place to talk. But it wasn't that I didn't want to see you; I just had some things to sort out. My sister...' He looked away.

Dorothy noticed a blonde woman standing a few feet away. She gave a small wave in their direction and Dorothy wondered if this was Philip's sister.

The crowd moved around the corner to the community centre and, once again, Jayden spoke to them: 'You can smell roasted chestnuts, because we have a roasted chestnut vendor here.'

Dorothy looked around to see the vendor, but she didn't feel hungry anymore.

'Why couldn't you tell me about your family?' she said aloud to Philip, not worrying who would hear. 'Why were you going to the station yesterday?'

She was more concerned with the answer to the latter question. It felt as if so many things were missing from this part of her relationship with the man standing next to her. She was fed up with him holding back on her.

The choir began a new song. '*Hark the Herald...*'

Dorothy sighed. She wasn't ready for this. The optimistic feeling she'd had when he first approached and shared his chips with her had vanished into the crisp night air, and frustration had replaced it.

'I missed you, Dorothy,' Philip said, attempting to keep his eyes level with hers while she looked away.

She shook her head and broke the connection. 'I don't know what's going on with you, Philip, but I don't need this. I want someone who's going to be open with me. Who's going to share their life with me. Not just bits of it. I don't want scraps; I want *you*. The full thing!'

With that, Dorothy shoved her song sheet into the hand of a teenager dressed in a blue choir cloak and stomped away, heading towards the field which led to the shortcut to her house.

She sighed as the vocalists ended their song and harked the angels this Christmas.

Chapter Eighteen

♥

Christmas Day

Christmas Day for Dorothy was usually a quiet day. In the past, she had gone to a film or for a long walk, but today she planned to stay in the house and bake. And she did just that. She barely stopped to go to the bathroom or eat. She simply snacked on the food she made. And every time she whisked the eggs, she put herself into it. Mostly to let out her anger through it.

'Stupid man!' she complained as she mixed the batter for the Swiss roll.

And she cried. Sometimes, she simply stood staring at the bowls of ingredients, tears running down her face, forgetting what she was meant to be doing next.

A couple of times she opened the door to her garden and stood quietly, looking at the wintery scene in front of her, her mind on Philip. Why couldn't he tell her the truth? Why didn't he tell her what was happening? And why hadn't she asked?

Later, she moved to savoury dishes. Mashing potatoes took the last of her disappointment. Then she laid the masher down on the side and placed the shepherd's pie in the oven.

Finally, at six o'clock in the evening, Dorothy settled onto the sofa in front of the TV, a plate of shepherd's pie and a cup of tea at hand. Finally, she had accepted it was time to stop things with Philip before she got well and truly hurt.

-x-

It was Boxing Day, and Dorothy had gone to the café to drop off all the things she had baked yesterday. Like déjà vu, as Dorothy closed the door to lock up the café, a dark blue car appeared on the road, pulling up as close as it could.

'There you are!' Philip's voice boomed out from it.

Dorothy didn't want to hear his voice. Not now, and not any time soon. She looked back towards the door and waited to hear the mechanical voice confirm that the security system was set.

Moments of her time with Philip floated through her mind. Sitting in the wine bar, talking in her café, walking hand-in-hand along the streets of Lavender Village. What had Philip called her?

A risk taker...

Another voice inside the car spoke, 'Philip, I'm going to miss my train!'

'Dorothy!' he repeated.

'Philip, please!' the voice said urgently.

Dorothy looked ahead. Words shuffled around her mind. She couldn't summon the exact sentences, but standing on the pavement, she felt tired of being pulled and pushed in other directions. She had found her strength, talking to that scowling man in her shop. She could find it again now.

Was she a risk taker? Yes! Did she have to speak to Philip now? No!

Dorothy continued down the pavement, her eyes focussed on straight ahead like a horse wearing blinkers. Another shout echoed in the air, but she didn't care. A protective layer wrapped around her, and she ignored him.

The car made a snappy turn and zoomed forward out of the village.

It took Dorothy several minutes to calm her heart as she stood outside the bookshop. Should she knock on the door and see if Oliver was in? The idea of sitting in the old, comforting rocking chair was appealing right now.

A mixture of feelings thundered through her. Hurt and pride. Two weeks ago, an incident like this would have given her a different feeling. Now, she felt strong. She knew she was capable of more, and a sense of satisfaction visited her.

What was she going to do now? Would she return to work tomorrow, or would she allow herself the pleasure of something different? A few days off, perhaps?

Strangely, hearing the word *train* gave Dorothy an idea. A new sense of hope pushed into her as she walked home, deciding not to bother Oliver.

As she walked, she took out her phone and made a quick call. After that, she quickly dialled another number.

'Half an hour? Yes, please,' she said into the phone.

Just as she hung up from the second call, her phone rang, an unfamiliar number appearing on the screen.

'Hello?' she answered.

'Dorothy!' Philip sounded tired.

'What do you want?' Her tone was direct and no-nonsense.

'To see you.'

'Well, you can't,' Dorothy said. 'I'm going away.'

'Where? Why?' Philip sounded frustrated. She could hear a muffled voice in the background.

'What do you want?' Dorothy asked again, nearing her house now.

'Please let me talk to you. We need to talk.'

'Philip, I'm not speaking to you right now. You are not going to push me into giving in.'

Dorothy hung up, a wash of pride filtering through her. She wasn't sure she'd ever spoken to anyone like that before. She unlocked her door and hurried inside, running upstairs to quickly pack her bag.

Chapter Nineteen

♥

Dorothy stared at the pink door of the stone cottage. She hadn't remembered it this way, but it had been decades since her visit. The visit where she'd had some of her most fun memories with her parents.

She remembered the white stone and coloured shutters – pink now, to match the door, though she was sure they had been blue last time she was here. She remembered her mother commenting on how the flowers over the door tied in the blue shutters.

Then there was the small bridge over the creek. She'd look for that later. She knew she couldn't re-enact everything, but she wanted to find a place where she could reflect and appreciate her parent's lives without the depth of the pain of loss.

-x-

Several days passed. Dorothy had planned to stay a week, but she soon began to feel different to how she had when she'd first arrived.

She didn't blame Philip anymore. When she thought of him now, she considered their date in the wine bar and the card he'd made and given her.

She remembered them scantily clad and running around her house. Twice!

Ridiculous, really.

And she remembered his effort at being 'a gentleman'. She'd liked that.

The day before New Year's Eve, Dorothy returned home earlier than planned. It was lunchtime, and as she stood at her open fridge, pondering what she would have to eat, she heard a light knock at the door.

She hesitated, thinking she'd just ignore it. No one knew she had come back early, so what did it matter if she didn't answer?

But then whoever it was knocked again. An even softer knock this time. She suspected it wasn't Philip; his would be louder.

With curiosity, Dorothy went to the door and was greeted by a stranger. 'Hello?'

The uninvited guest smiled. She held a small bag in her hand and wore a sheepish look. 'Hi, I'm—'

'Philip's sister?' she guessed, eyeing the younger woman. She had blonde hair, a prettily made-up oval face and was wearing a floaty dress and leggings, covered by a long coat.

'Connie, yes.'

Dorothy tried to remember what Philip had said about her. All she knew was she was younger than him and somewhat of a troublemaker.

'May I come in?' Connie asked.

'What are you doing here?' Dorothy questioned, though she stepped back to allow her entrance.

'Talking to you, I hope.'

'I was just making some lunch, do you want some?' Dorothy offered as they stood awkwardly in the hallway. She was visited by intrigue and the softness of wanting to help someone. Perhaps this meeting could get to the bottom of a few things.

'That would be kind,' Connie replied.

They moved to the kitchen and Dorothy approached the fridge again. As she busied herself making lunch, she asked, 'What are you doing here?'

Connie inhaled deeply. 'I came to talk to you.'

'Did Philip—'

'Philip doesn't know I'm here,' Connie interrupted, and Dorothy turned to her, surprised. 'I came by my own choice. I'm expected at some sort of party.'

'But you've got a bag.' Dorothy turned to look down the hallway at the overnight bag on the floor. 'So where are you staying?'

'I was going to go to the B&B after this, but I wanted to talk to you first.'

'The B&B is full. Unless you've already got a room there? It's always full this week.' She pulled out some celery and grapes, then turned back to Connie. 'Take your coat off.'

'Then I'll find somewhere else, or I'll stay with Philip in his room. Anyway, please can I talk to you?' Connie asked, an edge to her voice as she took off her coat.

'Yes,' Dorothy said, taking out a block of cheese. 'Could you grab the chopping board there, please?' She nodded towards a chopping board resting upright on the counter.

'Hold on, let me wash my hands,' Connie said. She did, then helped Dorothy to prepare the lunch.

Once the food was ready, they quietly sat together at the kitchen table.

'So, what's going on?' Dorothy asked, breaking the silence.

Connie's face relaxed a little. 'I want to explain about Philip and our relationship. I'm not telling you this to make you change your mind. Whatever you decide is your choice.'

Dorothy's eyebrows knitted together, but she nodded.

'I've always been the black sheep of the family. I've lived life on my terms. Philip learned loyalty; I learned freedom. When I was younger, I got into the wrong crowd and I needed money. Philip helped me out. I haven't really spoken to him properly since then.' She sighed. 'I was very flighty. I'd start a business, and he'd go and study it so he could help me learn how to run it. Over the years, I've ignored Philip's help, not saying anything more than *hi* occasionally. I've always sided with my mother, and he'd go with dad. So, when Dad died...' Connie paused. 'He told you about that?'

Dorothy remembered the conversation in the wine bar. She nodded.

'Well, Dad died. I stayed with Mum and we did the lot, funeral arrangements and everything. It wasn't pretty. Dad had some savings, but not a lot.'

Dorothy stayed quiet, wondering why she felt Connie wanted to tell her all this.

'After Dad died, I got pregnant,' Connie admitted.

Dorothy almost choked on a piece of celery. She cleared her throat and refocused.

'Why am I telling you this?' Connie asked, and Dorothy's head shifted to one side, as the question had crossed her mind. 'Two reasons. Firstly, I want my brother to know his nephew or niece. Secondly, Philip has changed this last week. He's become lighter and more fun. Kinder.' Connie paused. 'At least, he was for a while there, until you locked up your café. He was taking me back to the train station because I had a meeting I had to keep. An interview. I might go halves in a business, but that's another topic.'

'Hang on,' Dorothy said. 'You've been trying to call him, right? But he's ignored your calls.'

'Yes, he did for a while,' Connie said.

'Why do you want a relationship with him?' Dorothy asked. She didn't wait for an answer. 'And why do you want one with me?'

'Because he likes you,' Connie said. Her eyes were wide, her body leaning towards Dorothy. 'Since that argument you two had, he's been a grump.'

Dorothy sat back in her seat and took a long sip of her tea. 'He's going to have to sort out his own feelings. He's a grown man.'

Connie's face dimpled with a smile. 'Of course he is, and he will. But I need to know how much you like him. You went away. I know you did because the girl at your shop said you weren't expected back until the New Year. So, imagine my luck when I decided to pop down a little earlier to see Philip and I saw your lights on?'

'What are you actually asking me, Connie?' Dorothy set her mug down. 'If I'll get back with Philip, or if you'd like me to be a part of your family, too?' The second question felt a bit odd.

'Both.' Connie sat back, one hand on her protruding stomach.

'Oh,' Dorothy said. 'Why come to me and not him? You could use your influence to get him to change his mind.'

'He won't talk about you. He gets in a grump and shuts down.'

'Well, isn't that a sign it's over, then?' Dorothy wasn't sure she wanted to continue this discussion.

'No.' Connie looked at Dorothy. 'It's a sign he's deeply in love with you. He doesn't know how to express his feelings; that comment you made at the carolling was true. But you help with that. Besides, he talked to me about it after,' she added quietly.

Dorothy considered the other night. Not one of her finest moments, shouting across the crowd. What was it she had said? *I want you! The full thing*?

'What would happen if I no longer wanted any part of this or him?' she wondered.

'He'd get over it and we'd move on,' Connie said. 'He'll still be a part of mine and my child's life. I'll leave and—'

'You're not going anywhere.' Dorothy placed a gentle hand to the woman's wrist. She knew that Philip would be heartbroken if she did.

'You do like him,' Connie said softly. 'I saw that look when you opened the door.'

Dorothy smiled. 'I'm learning how to live my life with a partner. Those days away were... Well, I realised a few things. I need to tell him, though. Not you.' She paused. 'Connie, where did you sleep last time you were in town?'

'In a room at the B&B. There was one available,' Connie replied.

Dorothy sat quietly for several moments. She barely knew the woman, but she could hardly send Connie on her way, especially if there were no rooms at the B&B. She bit her lip. What she was about to offer was a risk, but if anything went wrong, she could always go back to Stephen and ask for his help.

'I've got an idea,' Dorothy said. 'You need somewhere to stay, and you can't go traipsing around the village in search of one.'

'I can make some phone calls,' Connie said.

'No.' Dorothy shook her head. 'I've got a spare room here. Stay here tonight, at least.'

Connie smiled back. 'I'd love that. Thank you.'

Dorothy rose and moved towards the woman. She outreached her arms and gave her a small hug. Heck, if she was going to be staying with her, she might as well move up the friendly scale.

-x-

Once lunch was cleared away and the kettle was boiling again, Dorothy heard another knock at the door.

'Dorothy! Glad you're back,' Oliver said as she swung the door open.

'Oliver, what are you doing here?'

'Checking to be sure you're back.' His eyes twinkled. 'Also to remind you to come to the soiree tomorrow night.'

'Soiree?' Dorothy asked, just as Connie appeared at the end of the passageway.

'Ah, Connie?' Oliver said. 'I didn't think you were coming until tomorrow.'

'Change of plan.' Dorothy gave him a smile.

'Will you both come tomorrow night then, please?' Oliver looked from one to the other. 'When can I expect answers?'

Dorothy looked to Connie and laughed. 'Now. Yeses from both of us.'

'Super.' Oliver had moved to turn around when Dorothy said, 'Oliver, would you like a cup of tea before you go?'

Oliver considered the invite for several seconds but shook his head. 'Thank you, but no. I'll see you both at the bookshop tomorrow. Eight o'clock!'

'Certainly,' Dorothy answered, bidding him goodbye.

She stood at the top of the steps and watched Oliver walk down the road slowly, relying heavily on his cane. She hoped he would be okay. Luckily the journey wasn't too far.

After he turned the corner, she closed the door and moved to where Connie sat on the sofa.

'So, how's the pregnancy going?' she asked her new friend.

Chapter Twenty

New Year's Eve

The next morning, Dorothy padded downstairs, well-rested from a great night's sleep. She'd slept so well, in fact, that she had forgotten somebody was staying with her, so when she stepped on the last stair and saw the light on, she froze. But seconds later, she remembered Connie was staying with her and relaxed.

She entered the kitchen to see Connie fully dressed and taking a mug from one of the hooks.

'Hello,' Dorothy said.

'Hey, how are you?' Connie replied. 'I hope you didn't mind but I set up your coffee machine, and I thought I'd do breakfast. As a thank you.'

'That's kind of you,' Dorothy said, remembering Philip telling her that Connie was a good cook. A mix of relief and interest visited her. 'How did you sleep?'

'Well, thanks. And you?'

Dorothy's smile widened. 'I slept great.'

'Coffee?' Connie asked.

'Yes, please.' Dorothy watched her pour it. 'So, do you enjoy cooking?'

'It's a secret pleasure of mine. Though I get lazy.' Her eyes shifted as if confessing a deep secret.

'It's unusual to have someone here to cook for me.' Dorothy paused. 'I'm really glad you came, Connie. Thank you.'

She meant it. The connection to Philip was one thing, but having this new friendship was the cherry on top.

Connie put the whisk down and moved over to Dorothy. 'So am I.' She reached over to rub her arm gently. 'Listen, in the event my brother doesn't get back with you, you'll still be my friend. Okay?'

Dorothy smiled sadly at the possibility and managed a nod. 'Will he be there tonight?'

'Probably. From what I know of Oliver Livingstone, it's highly likely the invitation is open to him, too.'

'Yeah.'

'So, have you got a plan for tonight?' Connie asked, setting a stack of freshly-cooked pancakes on the breakfast bar.

She didn't, but she wouldn't worry about that just yet. 'He'll have a double shock at seeing both of us,' she said.

Connie laughed.

'I want to bring something with me,' Dorothy decided. 'I have to get them from the café.'

'Those orange biscuits?' Connie asked. 'He'll love that.'

-x-

As Dorothy opened the door to the bookshop, a tornado of emotions whistled around her. The anticipation of spending time with her friends again and the fear of seeing Philip wrestled within her.

Would he accept her?

She swallowed back the bile. Since breakfast, she had barely eaten anything, and she wasn't sure if Oliver's invitation included food.

As it turned out, it did. She held the door open for Connie as they stepped into the bookshop, the smell of pizza hitting them.

'Hello there, ladies,' Oliver welcomed them.

'We're not late, are we?' Connie asked.

'Nope. Not at all,' Oliver said. 'My son is going to be late; my granddaughter got a little sidetracked with a film. And hunger, I suspect.'

Dorothy heard a movement behind her and looked towards the window. There she saw the outline of Philip's large body, just like she had the first day she'd met him.

'Hi,' she said.

'Hey,' he replied. 'How are you?'

'I'm okay.' Philip stepped forwards and Dorothy moved towards him.

Then his gaze shifted to the left and a shocked expression appeared on his face. 'Connie?'

Connie waved. 'Hi, Philip.'

'I thought you weren't coming until tomorrow.'

'Long story,' Connie said. 'I'll tell you later.'

Oliver stepped forwards with a plastic cup in his hands. 'Orange juice?' he offered.

'Oh, thanks.' Connie took the cup.

Philip's gaze moved back to Dorothy, who had now reached him.

'I think we should talk,' Dorothy said at the same time he blurted, 'I'm sorry.'

Dorothy smiled, waving a hand to let him speak first, and he gave her a grateful look.

'I'm sorry,' he repeated. 'Dorothy, I've had time to think, and I've missed you.' He held out a hand to her, and she accepted it. 'I was sitting in the rocking chair. I've done a lot of that lately. And I've realised that I want to be with you.'

Silence hung in the air for a second before Dorothy blurted, 'I want that too! I want you in my life. I want an "us".'

Philip let out a relieved breath before his arms wrapped around her and he squeezed her tight.

'I want you,' she continued, voice wavering. 'And I want to learn how to say no properly and better. But most of all, I want you.' She held up the cellophane package that was pressed between them. 'I got something for you, but it's probably a bit squished now.'

He laughed and loosened his hold on her slightly so he could grab the mug of orange biscuits. 'I'll still enjoy it.'

'I only brought one, so don't tell anyone,' Dorothy whispered conspiratorially.

Philip smiled and crushed his lips to hers. 'Now, let's sit in the chair. I feel better when I'm sitting in it – and with you.'

A few minutes later, from their spot in the rocking chair, they heard the rest of the guests arrive.

Abigail poked her head around the side of the shelves. 'Oh, thank heavens! I wasn't sure what to expect,' she said upon seeing them cuddled together. 'So glad I found the two of you canoodling.'

Dorothy glared at her friend. 'Let me introduce you to tact, shall I?'

Abigail brushed her off with a good-natured eye-roll, and Philip chuckled in her ear.

'No, really. Don't encourage her,' Dorothy said.

Dorothy settled into the evening, feeling the strength of love and friendship. Reviews of the Christmas Countdown were discussed, generally with good results.

'We'll be doing it again next year,' Oliver said. 'There might be some changes. Different coloured ink pads for Sprawling Green, and they might include more of their shops. But we still want to emphasise the village and get shoppers coming our way.' He chuckled.

Epilogue

♥

Eight Months Later

Dorothy opened the door of the bookshop and looked around excitedly, her eyes meeting Abigail's. Abigail pointed to Connie, who was inhaling loudly and staring at the carpet below her feet. Zara, Connie and Philip's mother, was comforting her.

'Everything is okay, Connie,' Isabel said, looking at Dorothy with a pained expression.

'I thought it was going to start at two o'clock in the morning,' Connie managed through her breaths. 'Not the afternoon!'

'Come on, the car's outside,' Dorothy said gently.

Connie moved forward a step. 'Is Philip impatient?' she asked. 'Don't want...' She took a deep breath. 'To get in a...'

'Stop,' Zara said, taking her daughter's arm. 'If Philip's impatient, I'll have a word with him. I'll tell him about *his* birth.'

Dorothy grinned and took Connie's other arm. They shuffled out of the door to a waiting (and very smiley) Philip, who held the car door open for his younger sister. Once Connie was settled, Dorothy and Zara took their seats in the back of the car.

Connie had asked Dorothy to be there when she gave birth, which made Dorothy cry every time she thought about it.

Several hours later, Connie welcomed a healthy baby, Alice, into the world.

-x-

Three months later, Dorothy cuddled Philip's baby niece, Alice. Waves of love washed over her.

Life had changed so much now that she was part of the Ray family. Her relationship with Philip was going well, and he had recently moved in with her and started a company to support the growth of small to medium-sized businesses in the area.

A few months ago, Oliver had started to complain that climbing the stairs to his flat was becoming too difficult, so it was decided he would move to the ground floor of the building, into the flat behind the bookshop. Previously it had partially been used for storage and as a rarely-used staff room and office, so this was a much more efficient use of the space.

In turn, Connie and Zara – who had decided to sell their houses in Manchester and move to Lavender Village – had rented the top floor of Oliver's flat and now lived there, along with baby Alice. There was plenty of space for the Rays and they kept a subtle look out for the bookshop owner, which Stephen found to be a relief, just in case anything happened to his elderly father.

'How's everyone doing?' Dorothy asked Connie. She was excited to be babysitting her goddaughter while Connie went to work. As she often did, Zara had travelled back to Manchester to visit her friends.

Though still taking things slow after the birth, Connie had started working in the café twice a week and continued her online bead and candle business in her spare time.

'Great,' enthused Connie.

Baby Alice cooed excitedly in Dorothy's arms, and they both laughed.

'Alice is very happy to have you here, it seems!' Connie said.

For an instant, Alice's expression reminded her of Philip, and she couldn't think of anything better in life.

Reviews are the lifeline of an author, could you take a couple of moments to post a sentence or two of your thoughts on this book?

Many thanks,

Caroline

About the author

Caroline McIntosh is an award-winning author. She earned a Red-Ribbon award from The Wishing Shelf Book Awards for her book, *The Wounds No One Sees*. Through her writing, Caroline pushes boundaries and believes in the wondrous qualities of love. Caroline's stories have a strong British influence, as she was born and raised there. She now lives in Canada with her husband and son.

Also by Caroline

The Lavender Village Series:

Romance In Lavender Village – when you sign up to my newsletter

A Fantasy Adventure

A Sparkling Love

A Returning Love

A Treasured Love

A Sweet Love – A Christmas Story

2 more exciting stories – which are being planned and titled

In The Night Series

A Standalone: The Wounds No One Sees

For more information: www.carolinemcintoshboooks.com

Milton Keynes UK
Ingram Content Group UK Ltd.
UKHW030915121124
451094UK00001B/39